Her So Called Husband

by
Chenell Parker

Text ChenellParker
to 22828 to be
added to my emailing list

Join my reader's group Chenell's Chatty Corner *on FaceBook*

WHEN IT COMES BACK AROUND

YOU'RE THE BEST PART

FEELING BLEU

Chapter 1

Man, I couldn't believe that I was back in this raggedy ass jail again. If somebody would have told me this a few months ago, I wouldn't have believed it. I'd been in the Jefferson Parish Prison for about two months now, waiting to be transferred to the Orleans Parish Prison.

Cherika didn't press charges on me, but I still had a probation hold for the gun that was found in my truck. I was supposed to have been transferred since last week, but I had to wait for them to send someone to come and get me.

Being in prison was no walk in the park, no matter where you were, but I would have much rather stayed where I was than to be sent to that hell hole in Orleans. That was the bottom of the barrel for real. I could hold my own, no matter where I went though.

Right now, I was sitting around playing cards with a few of the old heads while waiting for my upcoming visit. My pops and my brother, Eric, were bringing my kids to come see me today. I hadn't seen them since I got locked up and I was missing them like crazy. I just hated to be talking to them from behind a glass barrier. My brother told me that Cherika kept asking about visiting me. She claimed that she had to talk to me about something important. It probably had something to do with the divorce papers that I sent to her. If that was the case, no words were needed. All she had to do was sign and be done with it. I appreciated the fact that she didn't press charges on me, but I was still done with her trifling ass.

Alexus was another story. I tried to get my brother to call her, but she would never answer the phone. He and my pops went to the condo and all of her clothes and personal items were gone. She didn't waste any time moving on. I was hurt but, given the situation that I was in, there was nothing that I could do.

I knew that I shouldn't have been worried about her after the way she did me, but I couldn't help it. If we never got back together, that was cool with me, but I needed some answers before I could really move on. We never got a chance to talk before I got locked up, so I was never able to confront her about cheating on me.

Even after my brother and cousin told me that they saw her in the club with another man, I still had my doubts. That's the kind of hold she had on me. I'd had plenty of time to think since I'd been here and I realized that everything my mama and the rest of my family said about her was true. She did me the same way I did my wife. It was cool though; I could bounce back from anything, no matter what it was. Even a broken heart couldn't keep me down for long.

"Mack!" the guard yelled, getting my attention.

I stood up and walked over to where he was. I waited for him to call a few more inmates' names for their visits before we walked down the hallway towards the visitation area. My kids were the first ones I saw when I walked through the gate. They were jumping up and down, and I could tell that they were happy to see me. I felt like shit for putting them through this again. I smiled and waved at them as I went to take my seat. I almost pissed on myself when I saw who was with my pops and my brother.

Of all people, why would they bring that bitch, Cherika, to come see me? I didn't send her a visitation pass, so she must have used the one I sent to my mama or my sister. My brother saw the look on my face and motioned for me to pick up the phone so we could talk. I swear, if this glass wasn't separating us, I would have slapped that bitch in her mouth. Unless she was telling me that she signed the divorce papers, we didn't have a damn thing to talk about.

"I know that you're probably mad, but mama gave her the visitation pass to come see you. She said y'all need to talk about something important," Eric said.

"I just talked to you this morning and you couldn't tell me that?" I asked him. Before he could answer, my pops grabbed the phone and started talking.

"Look, I know this was an unexpected visit, but don't act a fool in front of these kids. They been looking forward to coming see you all week," he said.

He was right. They didn't need to see no more drama between me and their mama, so I figured the least I could do was hear her out.

"I'm good. Tell her let me talk to my kids first and I'll holler at her."

He handed my kids the phone and, one by one, they told me everything that I missed during the last few months. Drew was usually the quiet one, but he even had a lot to say. After a few minutes of hearing about school and everything else, my brother took the phone from them. They were upset, but my time would be up in a little while and I still didn't hear what it was that Cherika had to say.

"We gon' take them in the waiting room, so y'all can talk. Call me later bruh, love you," my brother said.

"Love you too man," I replied. I waved to my pops and my kids before turning my attention to Cherika. I didn't notice it at first, but she looked like she gained some weight. She lost a lot of weight the last time I saw her, but she picked it all back up and then some.

"What's up?" I asked her, getting right to the point. I really didn't want to talk to her at all, but I was curious about what she had to say that was so important.

"Um, we need to talk," she said, looking down at her hands.

"Ok, talk. I'm listening."

I'm not sure if I sounded as aggravated as I was. I didn't know why she was trying to be shy now. She was never shy before.

"I'm sorry about everything that happened," she stated.

I cut her off by holding my hand up in the air. It was no need for her to be sorry. The damage was already done.

"Sorry is not going to get me out of here so you can miss me with that. If that's all you came to say, you can leave." I stood to my feet, preparing to be escorted back to my dorm.

"No, that's not all that I came to say."

"Well, say something. You're wasting my time."

She was stalling and I was getting impatient.

"I'm pregnant," she blurted out.

I sat back down as she looked up at me while smiling. I didn't know what the hell she was smiling about because there wasn't a damn thing funny.

"I'm three months. I should find out what we're having next month," she continued.

"Wait, what the hell you mean we?" I know she wasn't trying to say that she was pregnant for me.

"We, as in me and you. I wasn't having sex with nobody else. Even before we had sex that last time, it's been a while for me."

"Man, you got me all the way fucked up. You fooled me once with Drew, but you won't get me again. You better go find your real baby daddy because it's not me," I said, pointing to myself.

"Are you serious right now?" She was looking at me sideways but I didn't give a damn.

"I'm dead ass serious. Before a few months ago, we ain't had sex in a minute and you want me to believe that you wasn't fucking anybody else? Fuck outta here with that shit!"

"Look, I admit that it was a possibility that Drew wasn't yours, but I know for a fact that this one is. We can take a test if you want to."

"The only reason why you're owning up to the situation with Drew is because you got caught. There's no telling how long you would have kept that lie going if you wouldn't have been forced to tell the truth. And you're damn right, we're taking a test before I sign anything! And since we're talking, what's up with those papers that you're supposed to be signing?"

"What about them?"

"What do you mean what about them? When are you planning on signing them?"

11

She stood up and looked me up and down before replying, "I'm not."

She slammed the phone down and walked away like everything was cool. I couldn't do nothing, being in the situation I was in, but I'd be damned if I played this game with her trifling ass again. I had to hurry up and get the fuck out of here to see what was really going on.

Later that night, I called and talked to my brother, Eric. I told him about Cherika claiming to be pregnant by me. I needed to know what he was hearing about all of that.

"She really is pregnant though. Erica went with her to her appointment the other day." That explained all the weight she gained, but I still wasn't convinced that I was the father.

"I don't doubt her being pregnant. I do doubt that her baby is mine though."

"Shit, I said the same thing. I didn't even know that you were still smashing that."

"Yeah, we did our thing a few months ago when me and Lex were into it. That still doesn't mean that she's pregnant for me."

I knew it wasn't impossible since I did have sex with her, but I still wasn't taking any chances with her ass. Cherika was conniving and I knew that better than anyone. She would do anything to get what she wanted and what she wanted was me.

"Well, she got mama and everybody else on board thinking that you're her baby's daddy. She's been over there every day."

This shit was getting crazier by the minute. When I got locked up, my mama and everybody else wanted a piece of Cherika's ass since she was the one who sent me here. Now, all of a sudden, they were in her corner once again. I was getting tired of talking about this shit, so I changed the subject.

"Man, I wish they hurry up and move me if that's what they're planning on doing. I'm trying to see what my probation officer gon' do with me," I told my brother.

"I know. Pops been calling up there every day, but he can never get in touch with him. But, aye, you know that nigga Quan is in jail over there in Orleans, huh? I talked to him the other day."

Quan was my hot headed lil cousin. He was one of them that got at that nigga Malik for me a few months ago at Pee-Wee's. Quan was usually the ring leader of everything that his crew did wrong, so he stayed in jail for one thing or another.

"Naw, I ain't know he was locked up again. Depending on where they put me, I might run into that nigga when I get over there."

Eric and I made small talk until the operator announced that my call would be ending soon.

"Alright lil brother, call me when you find out when they're transferring you," Eric said.

"I got you fam. I'll talk to you later," I replied before the phone hung up.

Four days later, I was on the transport van in route to the Orleans Parish Prison. I wasn't happy to be locked up, but I was happy that I would at least know what was up with me. I needed a release date or something to look forward to.

The van that I was in pulled up through a set of double gates and drove to the processing area at the rear of the building. Two guards came out and escorted me through a set of bars that led to the inmate intake area. As soon as the doors opened, the smell of mildew and piss assaulted my nostrils.

This was the one thing that I hated about this place. The upkeep was ridiculous. Even though it was jail, they kept it like the pound and treated all of us like dogs.

One of the guards told me to sit down while he took the shackles off my ankles. After that, he took off my cuffs and walked me to another area. The process for them to re-book me and issue me that dingy ass orange jumper took about 4 hours, which wasn't out of the ordinary for them. The intake clerks there were known to be the laziest bitches in the entire Louisiana prison system.

After what seemed like forever, I was finally being escorted to the dorm I was being housed in. It was so many niggas in there, it seemed like we would be sleeping on top of each other. I saw a few familiar faces that I recognized from my hood, so I nodded as I was being led down the hall. We stopped at an area that looked halfway decent compared to the rest of the jail, when the guard opened the cell and told me to go in.

I walked in and, of course, all eyes were on me. I started looking around to see if I saw any familiar faces in my temporary new home. This was definitely not what I was used to seeing in Jefferson Parish. They had a million C.O.'s over there, so you couldn't do nothing without getting caught. I didn't see one guard in sight when I looked around in this hot box.

I used to always hear that the inmates ran the prisons in Orleans Parish and that was looking like the truth. The inmates were playing cards, dominoes, and some of them were shooting dice. I made my way around to an area where a large group of men were standing. A huge smile appeared on my face when I saw a few dudes shooting dice on the floor in the back. My cousin, Quan, was in the middle of the game talking shit like he usually did when he was losing. His back was turned, so I walked over there and decided to fuck with him.

"Nigga, you always talking shit when you're losing," I said, smiling.

He jumped up and turned around to face me. Everybody was looking at us, thinking that they were about to see a fight. A few men, who I assumed were his goons, stood behind me like they were ready for something to pop off. Quan walked up to me and smiled as we embraced like we were long lost cousins, even though we saw each other just a few months ago.

"Man, I thought you were one of these scary ass niggas up in here. You was about to get your ass whipped," he said, laughing. "Eric just told me that you were being transferred, but he said he didn't know when."

His clique backed up after they saw that everything was all good.

"Yeah man, it took forever for them to send somebody to come get me."

"You know how slow these bastards are," he said as we walked off.

"Man, y'all got it like this in here?" I asked him while pointing at some of the things that was going on around us.

"Man, they don't care. As long as nobody dies, we can do what the fuck we want. These guards ain't trying to bring their scary asses in here for nothing."

Quan led me further into the dorm and started pointing out some members of his crew who got locked up with him. I remembered most of them from hanging with him when he was home. A few of them used to get their work from me, so we were real cool.

"You know Lil Mike crazy ass up in here too, huh?"

Lil Mike was a youngster that I used to run with when I first got out of jail. He was a wild child that was bout whatever and didn't have a problem laying a nigga down. If the price was right, he was in.

"Naw, I ain't seen that fool in a while."

We walked around the dorm, trying to see if we could find him. After asking a few people if they saw him, an older cat pointed him out to us. We spotted him talking to some more youngsters in a corner.

"Man, look who I found in this bitch!" Quan yelled to Mike as soon as we approached him. He looked up and pointed in my direction as he spoke.

"Man, I know that's not my dog!" Mike yelled as he walked over and gave me a one-arm hug. He had a huge smile on his face that mirrored the one on mine.

"What's been up lil brother?" I asked once we both settled down.

"Ain't shit. Just ready to get up out of here. I just asked your boy about you the other day. He just got transferred to this dorm too." It wasn't too many cats that I ran with, so I wanted to know who he was talking about.

"Who?" I asked as my curiosity got the best of me.

"He's over there," Lil Mike said, pointing to a group of men playing cards.

He was rambling on and on about something, but I couldn't tell what he was saying. My attention was focused on something much more important. After all these months with no signs of him, I had to get locked up to come face to face with that nigga, Troy, again. Shit was about to get real up in here.

"Man, I don't fuck with that nigga no more. As a matter of fact, I was about to get at his punk ass before he got locked up," I told him.

"What? The way he was talking, I thought it was all good with y'all."

"Nah, we're far from being all good," I said. I ran everything down to both men about what happened between me and Troy as we walked around the dormitory.

16

"So, this nigga stopped getting money behind a bitch?" Quan asked.

Quan and I were related, so he knew Cherika and Troy personally. He knew just like everybody else that I didn't give a damn about who she messed with because I was with Alexus.

"I guess so. You already know I wasn't tripping off that shit, but I guess he was. I would've respected him more if he would have owned up to it instead of acting like a broad. It was no love lost on my end."

"That nigga is lame as fuck for that. He be walking around here bragging like he was a boss on the streets," Lil Mike said, laughing. I had to laugh at that shit myself.

"How you a boss getting a first check and living in low income apartments?" I asked, shaking my head.

"Noooo!" Lil Mike yelled as he doubled over in laughter. I didn't mean to bust him out like that, but Troy was obviously in here pretending to be something that he never was. If it wasn't for Keanna, he would have been evicted a long time ago.

"Man, I'm done talking about that nigga; he ain't that important. What else do I need to know while I'm in here?" I asked both men as we continued walking. I already had one snake to watch out for. I needed to know how many more were in my presence.

Chapter 2

I looked down at my ringing phone and declined Eric's call for the fourth time today. I knew he had Dre on three-way because he kept leaving me voicemails. I wanted to talk to him, but I couldn't bring myself to answer the phone. I cried like a baby the first time I listened to the messages he left. After that, I deleted them all without even hearing what he had to say. Even though I missed him like crazy, I needed to get Dre and this entire relationship out of my system. I was happy for the first time in a long while and I wanted to stay that way.

I had so much to look forward to, with only a little over a year left in school. If it wasn't for Dre getting locked up, I know we would probably still be together. He wasn't the type of man who took no for an answer. I felt bad for turning my back on him, but I had to do this for me.

Everything that I had at the condo was moved to my mama's house since I never planned on going back. I gave the gate access card and door key to his brother because I knew Dre wouldn't have wanted me to give it to anybody else. I wasn't sure if he had money or something else of value somewhere in the house, so Eric was the only person I trusted with it. For once, I had to live my life the way I wanted to live it with no interference.

After driving with only my thoughts to keep me company, I pulled up to my destination and got out of the car. Before I had a chance to knock, the door was opened for me.

"Hey pretty girl," Tyra said, standing in the doorway.

"Hey Lady," I replied as I walked in.

Since Tyree and I had made things official a few months ago, I spent a lot of time with his mom and sisters. My best friend Jada, who was also Tyree and the twins' first cousin, would be with me most of the time. Lately, she had been locked up in her apartment with her new boo, so she didn't have time to hang with us as much as before.

"I guess Jada dropped out on me, huh?" Tyra asked, looking behind me.

"I don't know what's been up with her. I called to tell her that I was on my way, but she didn't answer."

Tyra and her husband were having some guests over so she asked me, Jada, and the twins to help her set things up before they arrived. And just like every other time since she got with her mystery man, Jada was a no show. I was kind of hurt by her actions. We were supposed to be best friends, but I had yet to meet the man in her life. Hell, I didn't even know his name. She always referred to him as her boo and left it at that. She got defensive whenever we asked about him, so we stopped asking.

"I've been meaning to tell you that I love that car honey," Tyra said, snapping her fingers.

I was happy to finally have a car. Tyree wanted to buy me one, but I refused to let him. Thanks to Dre, I had enough money saved up to do it on my own. After debating for about two weeks, we finally agreed to go half on it, but I made sure that everything was in my name. I had a sage green Nissan Maxima with peanut butter colored leather seats and wood grain paneling inside. Depending on other people for a ride was a thing of the past for me and I didn't miss it at all.

"Thanks, I love it too," I replied, smiling.

"Hey girl," Trina said, coming down the steps with two duffel bags.

"Let me put our bags in your car, so we don't forget them."

The twins and I were spending the night at Tyree's house when we were done helping Tyra. He had been trying to get me to move in with him, but I wasn't ready. I felt in my heart that Tyree was the one, but I didn't want to ruin it by moving too fast. He was upset but, at the end of the day, he had to respect my feelings. I still slept over there some nights, just to shut him up.

When I wasn't at his house, I stayed with my mama or Jada. For the past few days, I'd been by my mama since Jada always had company. My sister, Ayanna, had recently moved back home too since she lost her job. My mama was ready for them to go, but I thought it was fun being around the kids all the time.

Ayanna had recently started doing janitorial work at night, so one of us had to babysit most of the time. She worked all night and slept all day, so we had her kids more than we wanted to.

"Alright, y'all can come help me bring these decorations outside," Tyra said, snapping me back into the present.

She was doing a Luau theme since they were entertaining outside by the pool. Tyree and the twins' father, Mr. Tee, ordered the food and was waiting for it to be delivered. He picked the cake up a few minutes ago and was now putting ice in the ice chest.

"So, where did you order the food from daddy?" Tina asked.

"I ordered everything from Kayla's mama. She gave me a good price for it too. Somebody should be here to deliver everything a little later."

I noticed the look that was passed between Tyra and the twins. I didn't know what it was about, but I was sure I would find out soon enough.

About an hour later, we were done decorating and were now sitting in the kitchen eating ice cream straight from the bucket. I was just leaving Jada another voicemail when someone rang the doorbell.

"I got it," Tina said, getting up from the kitchen table. A few minutes later, she walked back in carrying a covered pan, followed by another woman. They made two more trips outside before they were done bringing everything in.

"What the hell did Mr. Tee order?" I asked. They had about eight covered dishes sitting on the kitchen counters, as well as two long pans on the table.

"Girl, I don't know, but that shit smells good as hell," Tina replied.

"It is good. You know my mama can cook," the unknown woman said, laughing.

"Hey Tyra," she said when Tyra walked into the kitchen.

"Hey Kayla," Tyra replied dryly.

So, this was Kayla. I didn't know her, but I knew that her mama owned the restaurant and catering business that Mr. Tee ordered the food from. She was a pretty girl, but she wore too much make-up. Her cocoa colored skin was beautiful against her hazel colored eyes. She was kind of heavy, but she had a nice figure to pull it off. I could also tell that the sew-in she wore had seen better days. It was tangled and completely dried out. Out of a possible ten, she was a five at best. I noticed that she kept looking at me like she wanted to say something, but she didn't until I ran my hand through my hair.

"What kind of hair is that?" Kayla asked, looking at me.

"Huh?" I countered, confused by her question.

"Girl, she must think that's fake hair in your head," Trina laughed.

"No boo, that's my sissy's real hair," Tina said with her hand on her hip.

"Your sissy?" Kayla asked Tina, while looking at me.

"Yes, my sissy, as in sister-in-law."

"Oh, Kayla, this is Alexus, Tyree's girlfriend. Lex this is Mikayla, a family friend. Her mother and I went to school together," Tyra said, introducing us and putting too much emphasis on the word 'girlfriend'.

"Oh, ok. I didn't know that Ty had a girlfriend. He never told me that," Kayla said like she talked to Tyree regularly.

I was pissed to say the least. Tyree was talking to this heifer and I didn't know anything about it. Until today, I never even heard of her before. And then the bitch was calling him 'Ty' like they had some kind of connection or something.

23

"Yeah, we just made it official a few months ago," I said, breaking my silence.

"Yeah, my big brother finally found the one," Trina said, slapping my arm.

She knew that I was mad just by looking me. I smiled to let her know that I was cool, but this was far from over. I couldn't wait to see his ass and rip him a new one. As if on cue, Tyree came strolling through the front door like he didn't have a care in the world. He walked into the kitchen and came straight to me, kissing my lips.

"What's up y'all?" he said as he pulled me out of my chair. He sat down and pulled me on his lap.

"Hey Ty," Kayla said, a little too sweet for my liking.

"What's up?" he said, still kissing all over my face and neck. I noticed the uncomfortable look on Kayla's face when he started kissing my neck and that really made me wonder about the extent of their relationship.

"Ugh, I hope you don't act like this when we get to your house. Let the damn girl breathe," Trina said.

"Shut up," Tyree replied.

"Well I'm about to get going. Good night everybody," Kayla said. I could tell that she didn't like our display of affection, but oh well.

"Good night, let me walk you outside," Tyra said, walking behind her to the front door. As soon as the front door closed, I got up and went in on Tyree's ass.

"So, we're keeping our relationship a secret now?" I asked him with fire in my eyes. "Let me know, so I can stop telling people that we're together," I said.

"Well, that's our cue; let's go Tina," Trina said, getting up from the table.

"No, y'all don't have to go; I'm leaving," I said, grabbing my car keys and purse.

"Man, you can't be serious. What the hell are you talking about?" Tyree said. I ignored him and continued to walk off. He stood up and pulled my arm, forcing me to come back.

"Let's go outside and talk."

"No, I'm going home. We don't have anything to talk about." I felt like crying, but I really didn't know why. I didn't have any proof that Tyree was talking to Kayla or anyone else, but my gut feeling told me that something was going on.

"That's your whole problem. You always run away from shit instead of talking about it. Stop being so damn childish," Tyree said, pulling me into him.

"Whatever, I'm about to go." I tried to pry his hand from around my waist.

"What's wrong with y'all?" Tyra asked when she came back into the kitchen.

"Nothing. Y'all can go ahead and drive her car to the house. Use the red key on the keyring to open the door. She gon' ride back with me." He grabbed my car keys out of my hand and threw them to his sister, Trina.

No, this nigga didn't give nobody my car. Trina drove my car before, but I was always in the passenger seat when she did. Tyree pulled me outside in the yard and walked me around back to the pool house. Once we were inside, he locked the door and turned to face me.

"Don't do that no more. I hate putting everybody in my business. If you want talk to me about something, don't do it front of everybody like that," he said in an angry tone. I didn't give a damn if he was mad. I was mad too.

"Whatever Tyree, or should I say Ty? It looks like everybody is already in your business from what I can see."

"What the hell that's supposed to mean?"

"Why you never told ole girl that you had a girlfriend?" I sat on a bar stool, waiting for him to answer.

"Who is ole girl, Kayla?"

"Yeah, Kayla," I replied sarcastically.

"Man, I don't talk to or see Kayla, so how can I tell her anything? I know that's not why you're mad," he said, looking down at me.

"That's exactly why. She said that you never told her you had a girlfriend, like y'all talk all the time or something. I already told you that I'm not into playing games. I did enough of that when I was with Dre."

He looked at me like I was stupid and I almost felt like I was. I should've kept that last part to myself, but it was too late.

"From day one, I've been honest with you about everything. I don't have shit to hide, so stop comparing me with the next nigga. I'm not Dre and no other nigga that you use to deal with. I'm Tyree, take it or leave it. And as far as Kayla goes, I fucked her a few times and that was that. We never had a relationship or nothing else. Don't come at me sideways about nothing; all you have to do is ask."

He told me off without even blinking an eye but that was nothing new. I couldn't say that I was shocked because Tyree was very outspoken. He didn't handle me with kid gloves like Dre did. He treated me like the grown ass woman that I was or claimed to be. He was right about everything that he said, so I didn't have a comeback. I sat there like a spoiled brat with my arms folded across my chest.

I really had to get myself together. Every man was not like Dre and I had to get that through my head. Tyree had never given me any reason to doubt him, but my insecurity was driving me crazy. I loved the fact that he had it all together. He had his degree, and he and his father had a booming real estate business that had him financially set for life. They both had huge houses and more than enough rental property to spare. I was scared of being hurt, but I didn't want to push him away with my accusations.

"Stop acting like a lil ass girl," Tyree said, sitting down next to me. He pulled me onto his lap and kissed me softly on my lips. "I love you, baby," Tyree said, melting my heart. That was all I needed to hear to set things off.

I responded by giving him a deep, passionate kiss. I moved my tongue in and out of his mouth while sucking on his bottom lip in between kisses. I moved my hands down and started unbuckling his belt. Tyree saw that I was having trouble, so he moved my hands and did it himself. He lifted his lower body up, allowing me to pull his pants and underwear down slightly. I reached my hand down in his boxers and pulled out his 10-inch monster. Tyree and I had sex many times, but my eyes still widened in surprise at how big he was. My hands were tiny, so I used both of them to massage up and down his shaft as we continued to tongue wrestle.

I felt Tyree reach under my dress and tug at the lace on my thong. I was about to help him, but he got impatient and ripped them off with one hard pull. I laughed because I knew how impatient he was when it came to sex. He hated to wait for it. Tyree and I could be anywhere but, when he wanted sex, he made a way to get it. Just like right now, we were in his parents' pool house and their company was due to arrive at any minute. Panic set in just that fast with me realizing what we were about to do.

"Tyree, wait. Your mama is about to have company. We need to finish this at your house," I said, out of breath.

"What! You must be crazy. Look at this," he said, pointing to his third leg. "I'm not going anywhere until you make it go down." He was laughing but I was really nervous.

"Baby, I'm serious. I don't want people looking at me walking out there with my hair all over my head and no underwear on."

"It's gone be quick, I promise. We'll be finish before anybody shows up if you come on," Tyree said. He stood up with me still in his arms. He let me down and I stood to my feet. He laid down on the sofa and motioned for me to come to him. When I got close, he grabbed me and lowered me down over his face, with us both facing the same way. I already knew what he wanted. Tyree loved the sixty-nine position. He was the first person that I ever gave oral sex to. I only knew what he taught me and he only taught me to do what he liked.

I leaned forward and immediately took him into my mouth and started sucking like my life depended on it. I wasn't a pro, so I only took in as much as I could stand. I had to be doing something right because Tyree was moaning like crazy in between the tongue bath that he was giving me. I moved my hips in a circular motion over his face, enjoying the sensation of his warm tongue. When he inserted his finger in my hot box, I thought I was going to go crazy. When he started sucking on my clit, I couldn't take it anymore and tried to get up.

"Stop trying to run from me," Tyree said as he pulled me back down and continued to suck.

"Ahh!" I screamed as my body started bucking wildly. Tyree still didn't let up, as I shook and trembled from the killer orgasm that he had just delivered. Before I had a chance to catch my breath, he pulled me down and slammed me onto his rock-hard dick.

"Oh shit," Tyree moaned as I bounced up and down on him in the reverse cowgirl position. This was his favorite position and I knew just what he liked. He gripped my hips firmly and slapped my ass cheeks as I bounced to my own rhythm. After a few minutes, I spun around to face him so that I could see the look on his face. He had his eyes closed, but the look on his face was that of pure pleasure.

"You ready to cum baby?" I asked him when he opened his eyes. We had been in here long enough and I was ready to end it before any of Tyra's guests arrived.

"Yeah," he responded, breathing hard and labored. I tightened my muscles and held on to his neck as I slid up and down his shaft as fast as I could.

"Damn Lex!" Tyree shouted as his eyes rolled back in his head. He started to get loud, so I covered his mouth with mine to shut him up just in case anybody was close by. He pulled my hair and bit hard into my neck as the sensation got to be too much for him.

"Fuck!" Tyree shouted as he shot what felt like a bucket load of cum inside of me. I was happy that I was on birth control because that was damn sure a baby that he just unloaded.

"Girl, you bout to make a nigga propose to your ass in here," Tyree said in between deep breaths.

"Boy, shut up. We need to hurry up and get out of here before all these people come." I sluggishly lifted myself off of him. I grabbed my purse to get my feminine wipes when I heard somebody fumbling with keys at the pool house door. Tyree jumped up and starting fixing his clothes.

"I told you that somebody was gon' come in here," I whispered to him while trying to fix my hair and clothes.

"Stop being so damn scary, we're grown. It ain't nothing that they never saw before."

Tyra opened the door and laughed when she saw us standing there looking guilty.

"I don't even want to know what y'all were doing in here, so I'm not going to ask. I just came to get some extra chairs."

29

"Yeah, we came in here to talk," Tyree said, smiling at me. I flipped my middle finger at him and continued fixing my hair.

"Yeah, me and your daddy come in here to talk sometimes too." Tyra laughed but Tyree didn't find anything funny.

"Man, don't nobody want to hear that. Let's go baby," he said, reaching out his hand for me.

"Nigga, how do you think you got here? And y'all forgot something while y'all were in here talking." She held up my torn underwear and I wanted to disappear.

My eyes bucked when I saw what she was holding up. I was too embarrassed for words. Tyree grabbed them out of her hand and stuffed them in his front pocket.

"Thank you and good night," he said, pulling me along after him.

"Don't be embarrassed girl. Y'all are still young, so enjoy it while you can," Tyra said to my departing back.

"That was too embarrassing." I dropped my head in shame once we were in the car.

"My mama knows what's up. You're my girl. It's not like you're some random chick that I fucked in her pool house," Tyree said, driving away from the house.

"How many random chicks have you fucked in her pool house?" I looked over at him, awaiting an answer.

"Please don't start with that foolishness. I have never had sex with nobody else in my mama's house or in her pool house, not even when I lived there. I promise, you are the first and only one that ever had it like that," he said, kissing my hand. I leaned over to the driver's side of the car and kissed him on the lips.

30

"That's all you had to say then," I laughed. He shook his head and laughed too as we made our way to his house where I knew we would be doing any and everything but sleeping tonight.

Chapter 3

It was only 7 a.m. on a Monday morning and I was already up. I was downstairs in my basement, preparing to get my work out in early since Alexus was still asleep. We had just gone to bed at about three, but I couldn't get back to sleep for nothing. My sisters stayed over with us for the weekend but, when they left last night, I begged Lex to stay. I loved waking up next to her in the morning, but she was adamant about not moving in with me.

Lex and I had been kicking it for a while, but we had just really made it official a few months ago. I already couldn't picture my life without her in it. She was the one; there was no doubt about that. Alexus was everything that I was taught to want in a woman and more. She was beautiful inside and out, not to mention how smart she was. Neither of us had kids and we had never been married. We were a perfect match.

Everywhere we went, people always said that we made the perfect couple since we complemented each other so well. To me, it felt like we knew each other longer than we actually did.

Our relationship wasn't perfect and I wasn't looking for it to be. We had problems just like any other couple. One of our problems was her insecurity. I knew all about her relationship with her married ex-boyfriend, Dre. He really had her messed up when it came to trusting other men. Honestly, it didn't bother me because I didn't have anything to hide. I just really wanted Alexus to trust me. I had a reputation for being a dog in the past, but that was a done deal. When Lex and I decided to make things official, I was done with everybody else. It pissed me off when she told me how Kayla was trying to start shit the other day at my mama's house. Before then, I hadn't seen her thirsty ass in a minute. She swore that she was gone be the one when I settled down, but she had the game all the way fucked up if she thought that.

Kayla was something like a stalker. My mama was cool with her family and that's how I met her. We did our thing a few times, but she got more out of it than I did. She ended up catching feelings and couldn't handle it when I didn't feel the same way. My sisters started hanging with her because she bought her way into a friendship with them. After a while, they didn't want to have anything else to do with her when they saw how clingy she was. My mama even had to stop her from showing up at her house unannounced. When I got rid of that headache, I never looked back.

It was the other way around with Alexus. I never wanted her to leave. She felt like we were moving too fast, but I didn't see it that way. This was the first time that I could actually say that I was in love with a woman. I knew that she felt the same way, but her past experiences were holding her back from giving me her all. It was a plus that my family loved her just as much as I did, and her family welcomed me with opened arms.

"What are you doing up so early?" Lex asked, standing behind me. I turned around and forgot all about working out when I saw her. This was one of the reasons I loved to wake up to her in the mornings. She wore some pink and black lace boy shorts with the matching lace tank top. Her body was the most perfect thing I'd ever seen. I was staring so hard; I didn't realize that I never answered her question.

"Helloooo." She snapped her fingers loudly to get my attention.

"Huh. I'm sorry baby. What did you say?"

"I guess you didn't hear me since you're too busy ass watching," she said, laughing.

"What do you expect when it's that big? That's the first thing I see when you walk in the room." I was laughing, but I was dead serious. Alexus had ass for days. A man would be stupid if he didn't stare.

"Whatever, I'm going back to bed. My first class doesn't start until five and it's too early to be up. We just went to bed a little while ago." She yawned while walking away.

"I know, but I couldn't sleep. You need to help me out with that." I picked her up and carried her up the stairs.

"Damn, I've been helping you out all night and most of the morning too."

She was right, but I couldn't help it. The sex was the shit and I couldn't deny that I was hooked. She didn't know too much about oral at first but, once I showed her what to do, it was all good from there. Once we got upstairs in the bedroom, I stripped down out of everything that I had on. As soon as I went to take Alexus' clothes off, my phone started ringing. I swear, if it wasn't my pops' ringtone, it would have gone straight to voicemail.

"Yeah!" I yelled into the speakerphone once I answered the call.

"Are you on your way?" he asked.

"On my way where?"

"We're supposed to be meeting with these contractors this morning or did you forget?"

Damn, I forgot all about the meetings we had going on today. The building that we leased to a nursing home was in need of some renovations and we were scouting out a good company to make the changes.

"No, I didn't forget," I lied. "I'm about to jump in the shower and I'll be on my way."

This was not a good time, but I had moves to make. I hung up the phone and got up from the bed.

"I gotta go baby," I told Alexus.

"Why, what's wrong?" she asked, concerned.

"We got some meetings set up for this morning. I forgot all about that shit." I hated to leave her, but I no choice.

"It's cool; we can hook up later after my last class," she said. Her last class was at nine tonight and that was too long for me to wait.

"Hell no, I can't wait that long. Come hop in the shower with me." I didn't wait for her to reply. I picked her up and led her to the shower for a quickie that would hold me over until later.

About three hours later, my pops and I were still meeting with contractors who we felt could do the job that we needed done. This was the part of my job that I hated. I could talk numbers and contracts all day, but I hated these boring ass meetings. My pops knew how I felt, but he stressed the importance of me knowing our business inside and out. I knew he was right and that was the only reason why I never skipped out on it. He always said that I would be running the business by myself when he retired, so I needed to take in everything.

My father was wise way beyond his 47 years of age. He didn't have a degree, but he had a mind for business. He made sure that I got my education so that I could go further than he did. I always appreciated him for that and so much more. It was because of him that I didn't have to work another day in my life if I didn't want to. The monthly income from all the real estate that I acquired was enough for me to live comfortably without touching what I had in the bank. That's why buying Alexus a car wasn't a big deal to me, even though she insisted on us going half on it. I had more than enough money to make sure she never wanted for anything. She didn't care about how much money I had and that was another reason why she had my heart. It was the little things that made her smile and that was rare.

"Alright, we have a little break in between our next meeting. You can go get you something to eat if you want to," my pops said, breaking me out of my trance. I was hungry, but I wanted to wait until I met up with Alexus later to get something to eat. The vending machines in the break room would have to do for now. I saw a familiar face as soon as I walked through the doors.

"Hey stranger," Keanna said as soon as she saw me.

"What's up?" I spoke back. I was used to running into Keanna whenever I had to visit the building since she worked there. She was cool, but I didn't know much about her outside of where she worked. I was shocked to find out that she knew my girl because it didn't look like they ran in the same circle.

"I'm so happy that y'all are fixing this place up. The people who had it before didn't give a damn if it was falling apart," she said. I was on the phone trying to call Alexus, so I wasn't paying much attention to what she was saying. This was my second time calling, but I kept getting her voicemail. I guess she was still tired from me keeping her up all night.

"You heard me?" Keanna asked.

"My fault; what were you saying?"

"I was saying how happy I am that y'all are fixing this place up. But anyway, how are you and Lex doing?"

"We're good," I replied. I wasn't the type to talk about my personal life with anyone and she was no exception to that rule.

"That's what's up. At least she don't have to worry about my cousin interfering in y'all relationship. I know she happy that he's locked up." That got my attention even though I tried to play it off.

"Who is your cousin?" I asked as I turned to face her. She had an awkward look on her face when she answered.

"Oh, I thought you knew that Dre and I were first cousins. My fault, but please don't tell her I told you."

This was all news to me. When they saw each other at the club, I asked Alexus how she knew Keanna and she only said they went to school together. It was never mentioned about her being related to her ex. I was just about to respond when the break room door swung open. Alexus walked in carrying a plate of food in one hand and a drink in the other.

"Hey baby. I just went upstairs looking for you. Mr. Tee told me you might be down here," she said when she entered the room. This was one of the reasons why I wanted to wife her. She was always looking out for me, even when I wasn't looking out for myself.

"I was just calling you," I said, walking up to give her a kiss.

"I know, but I was already on my way." She sat down at the table right next to me.

"Hey girl; I was just asking about you a minute ago," Keanna said to Lex.

"Hey girl; what's up?" Lex responded.

"What are you doing here?" I couldn't help but notice the way that Keanna looked her up and down when she asked the question.

"I came to bring my man something to eat." Lex gave her a look like she dared her to say anything.

"Oh ok. Are you here with Jada?"

"Nope, I'm here by myself in my own car. You are nosey as hell." Lex laughed but I could tell that she was serious.

"Girl, you finally bought you a car huh?" Keanna asked her, laughing in return. I caught the sarcasm in her voice, but I didn't think Lex paid attention to it.

"Yes, I finally got a car and I couldn't be happier," she said, looking up at me while smiling.

I pulled her up from her chair and sat her on my lap. Maybe I was tripping, but I thought I saw Keanna frown up a little when she saw that. Alexus opened the plate of food she brought for me and starting feeding me while we talked. This time, there was no mistaking the scowl that Keanna wore. I didn't know what her problem was but, if I had to guess, I would say it was jealousy.

"What's up with you and Jada? When was the last time y'all talked?" Keanna asked Lex.

Jada had been on some bullshit lately. I didn't like how she put everybody on the back burner just because she got with some new nigga. I especially felt some kind of way about how she was ignoring my girl. I was making it my business to call her out on it the next time I saw her. Her and Lex were way too close and that was not like her at all.

"We're alright; I haven't talked to her in a few days," Lex replied.

"I'm shocked. Y'all are partners in crime," Keanna said. For some reason, she sounded happy about it. According to Lex, Keanna and Jada hated each other, so I was surprised that she was so concerned with her whereabouts.

"We still are, but she's been spending time with her new man and I've been spending time with mine," Lex replied. I knew my girl was hurt about how Jada had been acting lately. They were very close and you rarely saw one without the other.

"Her new man, huh?" Keanna said with a smirk on her face. It was something about her that I couldn't quite figure out. It was almost as if everything she said had a double meaning. I really wanted to talk to Alexus about a few things, but I wouldn't say anything as long as she was around.

Chapter 4

I gotta go baby," Tyree announced after he ate his food.

"Awww," Alexus whined.

Ugh. I really couldn't believe this prissy bitch was sitting here pouting like a little ass girl. I felt like throwing up watching them kiss and feed each other like newlyweds, so I was happy that he was leaving. Alexus was an undercover hoe, but I was the only one who seemed to notice. She had Dre wrapped around her finger and it looked like Tyree was about to be the same way. I knew she never told Tyree that Dre and I were first cousins, so I did it for her. They couldn't see that gold digger for what she really was. It pissed me off to see her sitting here dressed to kill like she had a nine to five, knowing that she never worked a day in her life. They didn't say, but I knew he was probably the one who bought her that car. Alexus was the type of woman who was used to having everything handed to her. She never had to experience working to get what she wanted.

I always had a job and sometimes two, ever since I was sixteen years old and still couldn't manage to get out of the hole that I always seemed to be in. My aunties always told me that a man would forever be my downfall, just like my mama. My mama died of a drug overdose when I was five years old, so I didn't remember too much about her. The man that she was living with got her hooked on heroine. When he got locked up, she started prostituting to get money for her drugs. She never had time for me, so I was always raised around my father's family. When he got killed a year later, my uncle EJ and the rest of my family took me in and made sure that I was straight. It seemed like no matter what they did for me, I still wasn't happy. Something was missing from my life, but I didn't know what it was. I was miserable and I hated to see when the people around me weren't.

Jada was living a lie too. She had a million skeletons in her closet that had yet to be exposed. I knew Jada long before I met Alexus but, when she came along, Jada forgot all about me and our friendship.

"Girl, I didn't know that y'all were that serious," I said to Alexus once Tyree left.

"Yes, we are." She had a huge smile on her face and I couldn't wait to slap that shit right off.

"Girl, Dre is going to lose his mind. You know how he feels about you."

Her smile faded instantly and was replaced with a look that I couldn't figure out.

"Girl, fuck Dre!" she said, sounding pissed. "He got a wife and kids that he should be worrying about, not me."

I was just like a tape recorder, memorizing everything that she said. My break was over 15 minutes ago, but I didn't want to miss anything.

"It was already over for me and Dre. I just didn't get a chance to tell him." She stood to her feet like she was preparing to leave.

"Girl, you have to do whatever makes you happy."

"I already know and that's exactly what I'm doing." She grabbed her purse from the table and headed for the door with me close behind her.

"I have class in a little while, so I'm out of here."

"Well, hopefully, I'll talk to you later."

We walked out together and went our separate ways. I needed to get in contact with Eric to see what was going on with Dre. I couldn't wait until he came home. I knew that I could count on him to help me end this thing between Alexus and Tyree. He loved Alexus to no end and would do anything to be with her. I needed to use that to my advantage.

I still wanted Tyree and I planned to get him one way or another. I didn't care that I had a man. Troy was still locked up so he couldn't do anything for me. He ended up having to do six months since I couldn't come up with the bail money that he needed. I had somebody else occupying my time right now, so I didn't care when he got out. I was really feeling my new boo, but I would drop him in a heartbeat to be with Tyree. Besides, he wasn't ready for anyone to know about us just yet and I blamed Alexus for that too.

It was about 10:30 when I pulled up to my apartments. I stripped down out of my uniform and left a trail of clothes behind me as I headed upstairs to take a nice long bath. I had been at work since six that morning and I worked a double shift, getting off at ten that night. Needless to say, I was tired as hell. I ran me a steaming hot bath and added mint-scented

Epsom salt to soothe my aching bones. I grabbed a night shirt and prepared to soak for a while.

As soon as I sat down in the tub, my phone started ringing. As usual, Troy always called at the wrong time. It was a good thing I had the phone in the bathroom with me or he would have gotten the voicemail. I was tempted to ignore his call, but I knew he would call all night until he reached me.

"Hey baby," I answered while trying to sound excited even though I wasn't.

"Don't fucking hey baby me!" he yelled. "What happened to the money that you were supposed to put in my account?"

After working sixteen hours straight, this was the last thing that I needed. He acted like my world revolved around his ass.

"Troy, I worked sixteen hours today. I didn't have time to do it. I'm off tomorrow, so I'll make sure it gets done then if that's alright with you," I said with an attitude.

"Bitch, you're always trying to get smart. I keep telling you that I'm not in here for life. That's the least you can do since you left me in here for six months." He was always trying to make me feel guilty.

"I'm not trying to get smart. I just didn't have time to do it today." I quickly humbled myself. I needed Troy for several reasons and I wasn't trying to make matters worse with him.

The low-income apartments that we lived in were very nice, but it was all his. My name was nowhere on the lease. Without him, I wouldn't even have a place to live. Living with one of my aunts or uncles was out of the question. I would rather stay here and take an occasional ass whooping from Troy before I asked them for help. They belittled me enough when I was a little girl.

"Your punk ass cousin got transferred up here a few days ago," Troy said, changing the subject out of the blue. That was music to my ears. Eric told me that Dre was waiting to be transferred, but he didn't know when it would happen. The department of corrections was slow as hell about things like that.

"Did y'all say anything to each other?" It was a stupid question, but I was curious.

"Fuck outta here with that bullshit! Me and that nigga ain't got shit to say to each other."

This nigga was a hot ass mess. He slept with Dre's wife, but he had the nerve to be pissed off with him. Usually, I would let Troy's comments slide, but I had to speak up this time.

"You act like he did you something. You're the one who slept with his wife." I knew that he was about to blow up so I braced myself for it. Troy hated when I took someone else side over his so I knew that he wasn't too pleased by what I'd said.

"This ain't got shit to do with that hood rat bitch he married. That nigga used to walk around like he was God or something. He was eating damn good, while he fed everybody else crumbs. Fuck that nigga and anybody that rock with his fake ass!"

So, that was it; he was jealous of Dre. I always knew that he was, but he just confirmed it for me. He was a hater.

"You were getting money too, so I don't see what the problem was." I was pushing it, but I didn't care. No matter how he felt about it, Dre was still my family.

"Man, I wasn't seeing half of what that nigga was seeing. And why the fuck are you acting like you're this nigga's cheerleader or something? Whose side are you really on?"

"Don't get mad with me. I'm always on your side; I'm just stating the facts." Now I had to speak up in my own defense.

"Fuck you, Keanna. I see where your loyalty at and it's not with me. Just make sure you put that money on my books tomorrow and make sure you come up her next week for visit," he said before hanging up.

I was so tired of Troy disrespecting me, but that was my own fault. When it started, I should have stopped it. It was too far gone for me to do anything about it now. I needed to really get myself together and try to get a place of my own because Troy always held that over my head. He would threaten to put me out every time things didn't go his way. I knew that would never happen because I paid all the bills in the house. Even though the rent was cheap, I still paid it, along with the lights, cable, cellphone, and car insurance bills.

I was stupid enough to sign for a truck for Troy and ended up getting stuck with another car note when he stopped paying the bill. It was three months behind, so it was only a matter of time before they came and picked it up. I knew he was going to have a fit when that happened. When he parted ways with Dre, it was over for him in more ways than one.

I added some more hot water to my bath and leaned my head back on my bath pillow. I dialed my boo's number and put the call on speakerphone.

"Yeah," he answered dryly.

"What's wrong with you?" I asked once I heard how he sounded.

"I'm good. What's up?" He didn't sound like he wanted to be bothered, but I wanted some company.

"Are you coming to see me tonight?"

"I'll pass. I'm in for the night," he said, crushing my hopes of getting some.

"Well, damn. You didn't have to say it like that."

"There you go. You always bitching." He sounded annoyed but he wasn't the only one.

"I don't care. I'm getting tired of this one-sided ass relationship that we have."

He breathed heavily into the phone before he spoke.

"Look, you knew what it was when we started but, if you're tired, feel free to walk away."

I was just about to respond when I realized that he had already hung up. This secret lovers shit was for the birds. It wasn't that serious. But he was right; I could walk away at any time. I just didn't know if I was ready to.

Chapter 5

This baby was kicking my ass. If I wasn't sleeping, I was eating up everything in sight. I gained so much weight it was ridiculous. I was almost four months pregnant but, if I kept eating like this, I was going to be big as a house.

I was happy about this pregnancy for so many reasons. For one, I knew without a doubt that my husband was the father. He was the only person that I had sex within the last year. I know he had doubts about the paternity, but a simple DNA test would solve that.

Dre and I had sex all day every day when he stayed at my house a few months ago. The first day, we didn't use any protection at all. After that, Dre refused to touch me without putting a condom on. He made a huge mistake when he didn't bring any of his own. We ended up using the ones that I kept in the medicine cabinet in my bathroom. That was a mistake that he would spend the next 18 years of his life paying for since every single one in the box had been tampered with.

When Dre was on his way over to bring our son some medicine, I put my plan in action. I used a stick pin to put holes in the entire box of condoms. Dre was weak when it came to sex, especially oral, so I knew all I had to do was give him some bomb ass head and the rest would be history. I was skeptical about doing it at first, but everything worked out perfectly. I was having his baby again and he would just have to get used to the idea.

I sat at my vanity mirror and started pulling the rollers from my hair. I had a meeting with Dre's probation officer in an hour and I did not want to be late. I didn't put any make-up on because I planned to do a lot of crying when I got over there. Erica and I set up this meeting to try and convince him to release the probation hold that he had on Dre. This pregnancy was the perfect reason for him to let my husband come home.

I was convinced that Dre would come back home to me, especially since Alexus had moved on. Erica told me about her moving all her stuff out of their condo and not answering any of his calls. I loved my husband to death, but that was so good for his dog ass. He fucked over me big time for Alexus and look at what she did to him. She was flaunting her new man around like she didn't have a care in the world. We all tried to tell him, but he never wanted to listen. Now, he saw who really had his back and it wasn't her home wrecking ass.

I looked down at my ringing phone and saw that Erica was calling me.

"Hey chick," I said, picking up the phone.

"I'm on my way, so I hope your fat ass is ready," she said, laughing.

"Whatever heifer, I'm almost done with my hair so I should be done by the time you get here."

"Alright, I'll blow when I'm downstairs," she said before hanging up the phone. I was so happy that I was back on speaking terms with Dre's family. They were mad with me for a while because I sent Dre to jail. When they heard what really happened and saw my black eye, they came around a little. Once everybody found out I was pregnant, they really welcomed me back with opened arms. i was so happy because their support meant the world to me. Eric and Dre's father still didn't care for me too much. I, along with Dre's mom, had to practically beg them to let me visit him. They didn't care that he gave me a black eye or treated me like shit. The fact that I sent him to jail was unforgivable to them.

I made my way downstairs and out the front door when I heard Erica's horn blowing.

"I'm about to win me an Academy award today boo," I said to Erica as I got in the car.

"Girl, I hope I don't laugh at your crazy ass. I know you're about to perform."

She was absolutely right. I could cry at the drop of a hat. It didn't matter what anybody said. If crying could get Dre out of jail, I was about to cry a river.

"Well, let me warn you now before you get surprised," Erica said, looking at me. I made eye contact with her and nodded, giving her the green light to keep talking. From the look on her face, I could tell that the news she was about to deliver wasn't good.

"Eric and my daddy are supposed to be meeting us up there, so don't be shocked if they do all the talking," she informed me.

My first mind wanted to tell her to bring me back home, but I decided against it. I was about to be in the presence of the two people who hated me the most, but my husband was worth it. My heart was beating at a rapid pace and I felt the sweat building up in the palms of my hands. I was a nervous wreck and we hadn't even gotten to the office yet.

"Girl, calm down," Erica said. I guess she noticed the change in my demeanor. Being calm would be easier said than done.

"I'm as calm as I can be. I'm trying to prepare myself, since I know they gone try to front on me in here."

"You know Dre don't do no wrong to them, but I got your back," Erica said, making me feel a little better.

"Thanks sissy, I appreciate that." I smiled but I was still nervous.

We drove for another ten minutes before we pulled up to the building that housed Dre's probation officer's office. I'd been here with Dre before, but that was only for him to pay his monthly fee. Erica and I got out of the car and walked up to the front door. My stomach was in knots, and I didn't know if it was the baby or my nerves. Erica grabbed my hand and led me to the elevators.

"Rika, do not go in here and be scared to speak your mind. Don't let my daddy and Eric intimidate you," Erica said as we made our way up the elevator to the 10th floor. Mr. Gibson, Dre's probation officer, was expecting us at 10:30, so we were about 20 minutes early. I looked around the waiting room for any signs of Eric and EJ.

"Thank God we got here before them," I whispered to Erica before I sat down.

"You are too scary." She laughed as she checked us in with the receptionist. If I had any luck, they wouldn't show up at all.

"She said he's back there with somebody else, but he should be almost done. We're his next appointment," Erica said while sitting down next to me. The waiting room was fairly empty, with the exception of 4 other people. There was a total of five probation officers here, so they were probably waiting for someone else.

"I'm just ready to get this over with. Dre needs to be home before this baby is born." I rubbed my rounding belly for emphasis. Besides the weight that I gained, nobody outside of my family could tell that I was pregnant. My breast, ass, and hips were the only things that seemed to get bigger. My belly had formed a little pouch, but I had to be naked for anyone to notice it. I loved being pregnant, but I missed my long island iced teas and Heinekens.

"Cherika Mack!" the receptionist called after about a 15-minute wait.

"Yes," I answered as Erica and I approached her desk.

"Mr. Gibson is ready to see you now," she said. She buzzed us through the door and told us to go to room 114. I became more nervous with every step I took, but I tried not to let it show. Erica walked in first with me trailing right behind her.

"Good morning ladies. Sorry to keep you waiting so long," Mr. Gibson said, shaking both our hands. He was a very handsome older gentleman with graying hair and a graying beard to match.

"That's okay. Thank you for meeting with us," Erica said in return. I was so relieved that we were able to get in here and talk to him without EJ and Eric interfering.

"No problem. So, you all are here on behalf of D'Andre Mack, right?" he asked, looking at me and Erica for confirmation. We were about to answer when his desk phone started ringing.

"Excuse me one moment please," Mr. Gibson said before picking up his phone. He briefly spoke to whoever was on the other end before disconnecting the call. He got up from his desk and went to open his office door. My breath was caught in my throat when I saw EJ and Eric come strolling in. I noticed the frown on EJ's face as soon as he saw me and I knew that this was about to be a complete mess. He and Eric sat in the chairs on the opposite side of me and Erica. They didn't even speak to her, so I know it was out of the question for them to say anything to me.

"So, let's talk about what everyone is here for today," Mr. Gibson said, looking around the room at all of us.

"I'm here-" I started talking but was rudely interrupted by EJ.

"I'm here on behalf of my son, D'Andre Mack. He was arrested a couple of months ago on a battery charge, but now he has a probation hold on him. Before this incident, my son stayed out of trouble. He paid you on time and he checked in every time he was supposed to. I just want to know what we can do to get him out of jail without being violated."

Mr. Gibson got up and walked over to his file cabinet and looked through some things before pulling out a manila folder.

"I made plans to go visit Mr. Mack next week. Let me look at what we have here," he said while reading over the paperwork. We sat quietly as he looked up some things on his computer. The tension in the room was thick enough to suffocate us all.

"So, he was arrested for battery on his wife?" Mr. Gibson asked. I wanted to disappear when EJ and Eric looked over at me.

"I'm his wife, but I didn't press charges on him, so I don't understand why he's still in there," I hurriedly corrected.

"The law doesn't work that way and he's in there for several reasons. For one, he had a gun in the vehicle that he was driving. Under the terms of his probation, he is not supposed to be anywhere near weapons," Mr. Gibson stated. This meeting was not going the way I thought it would go. I was getting discouraged with every word he spoke.

"What did you think would be the outcome of you calling the police on him?" he said, looking to me for an answer.

"That's exactly my point," Eric said.

"You provoked the fight and then called the police when he tried to defend himself. You hit him in the head with an astray or did you forget to mention that to the police?" EJ said.

I wasn't about to let them gang up on me and Erica didn't have my back as much as she said she did. She sat there in silence as her family went in on me about any and everything they could think of.

"Look, I'm not saying that I was right for calling the police on Dre because I did hit him first. Mr. Gibson, Dre and I have four kids together and one on the way. I need my husband home. I can't do this without him."

I started crying while looking over at him. I prayed that my tears were realistic. I needed this to work more than anything.

"So, he hit you while you were pregnant?" Mr. Gibson asked in shock. This meeting was going from bad to worse in a matter of minutes.

"We didn't know that I was expecting at the time," I said, wiping my teary eyes. At first I was forcing myself to cry, but now the tears were pouring for real. I would never forgive myself if Dre didn't come home before the two and a half years that he was facing.

"They only have three kids together and my son is not sure that he is the father of the unborn baby. He and Cherika were in the process of getting a divorce when he was arrested," EJ chimed in.

"That is a damn lie!" I shouted while standing to my feet. I couldn't believe that he was stooping so low. Dre was most definitely the father of my baby and I couldn't wait to

55

prove it to him and his entire family. And for him to exclude Drew as being Dre's child was just dirty. He was the only father that my son knew.

"Calm down Rika. Let's just try to get through this meeting without starting an argument," Erica said, grabbing my arm. I pulled away from her and sat back in my seat.

"Daddy, that is not true. They were not in the process of getting a divorce. He was still sleeping with her," Erica said. I was happy that she finally found her voice.

"It don't matter Erica; he wanted a divorce and that's why she sent him to jail," Eric said.

I was livid. I knew they were going to try to make me look bad and that's exactly what they were doing now.

"Okay, let's just calm down," Mr. Gibson said.

"I need to look over a few things before I can make a decision on what's going to happen with D'Andre. I haven't even spoken to him yet. Hopefully, I can pay him a visit sometime next week. I'll leave it up to him to tell everybody the outcome of our meeting."

He stood up from his desk and opened his office door. We all stood up too since we knew that was our cue to leave.

"Can I talk to you alone for a minute?" EJ asked Mr. Gibson before we left.

"Yes, you can have a seat at my desk," he said as he walked us out to the front lobby. I could only imagine what that conversation was going to be about. I rushed past Eric and Erica and pressed the down button on the elevator. I was ready to get as far away from this place as I possibly could.

Erica was lagging behind, talking to her brother. That was fine with me because I didn't want to be in the elevator with his no-good ass anyway. As soon as the doors opened, I pressed the close button and took the ride down by myself.

When I got off, I walked to Erica's car and waited for her to get there. This day was a complete disaster, thanks to Dre's father and brother. Erica and I were supposed to be going out to eat but, after this mess, I just wanted to go home and get in my bed.

Erica came out of the building after about five minutes, but Eric wasn't with her. That was good since I didn't care if I ever saw him again or not.

"Just bring me home. I'm not in the mood to go out to eat," I said when she approached the car.

"Why? I think you did good there." She smiled at me but I didn't return the gesture.

"You can't be serious. Your daddy and your brother ripped me a new asshole in there. All the shit Dre did to me don't even matter to nobody but, the minute I fuck up once, everybody is ready to hang me." I was tired of always coming up short when it came to Dre's family.

"We need to go somewhere and talk. I know you have a lot on your mind," Erica said as we got into the car. She was right. I had a shitload of things on my mind, but she couldn't help me with any of it.

"Where do you want to go?" she asked as she pulled off. I really wanted to go home but being by myself was not something I was looking forward to right now. My kids were with my sisters and they weren't coming home until tomorrow. Before I could answer her question, my emotions got the best of me and I broke down crying. Why did loving my husband so much have to be this complicated? I thought that was what a wife was supposed to do but, obviously, I was doing something wrong.

"Don't cry Rika, everything is going to work itself out." Erica tried her best to comfort me. I wanted to believe her. I needed to believe her, but it was too hard.

Chapter 6

A week later and I was still sitting in jail. I felt a little better since I knew that my probation officer was coming to see me soon. Eric told me about the meeting they had with him not too long ago. I didn't know what the hell Cherika was there for since it was her fault that I was sitting in here. Erica didn't even need to be there since she seemed to be on Cherika's side all of a sudden. I planned to check her ass too whenever I called my mama's house.

Being in here wasn't as bad as I thought it would be. Quan and Lil Mike kept the action coming all day, every day. I saw that clown Troy all the time, but he made sure to stay out of my way. I was focused on getting out of here as soon as possible, so he was the least of my worries.

I sat on my bunk waiting for the guards to call us to go

on the yard. I went on the yard every day to play basketball with my cousin and some of his boys. That made my days pass away a little faster. After a few hours of that, I didn't want to do nothing but take a shower and eat. It didn't matter if I stayed in or went out since it was hot as hell both places.

I saw Quan and Lil Mike headed my way with a few other dudes so I figured it was time to go.

"What's up lil cuz?" I asked as he approached me.

"Nothing but check it; you need to stay inside today," he said, whispering in my ear.

"Why, what's going on?" I looked at him and Lil Mike and could tell that they were up to something.

"Just trust me, fam. One day inside isn't going to kill you," he replied with a smirk.

"We got this, just trust us," Lil Mike said.

"Man, y'all lil niggas are always into some shit. Don't get caught up while y'all playing with these people," I warned.

Punishment in here was worse than actually coming here. We called it the hole because that's what it felt like, the bottoms. They put you in a small concrete room with nothing but a toilet, sink, and mattress for twenty-three hours a day. That alone was enough to drive anybody crazy.

"I'm going play cards. I don't need any parts of the bullshit y'all got going on."

I was trying to get out of here and I didn't need anything holding me back. I walked over by some of the older men and sat down with them. They never got into anything because they played cards all day. Maybe if I stayed close to them, I wouldn't get into anything either.

I watched as Quan and Lil Mike, along with some more inmates, made their way to the door that led outside. Troy walked past me, preparing to go out as well. I wanted to change my mind and go out there since he was going, but I listened to my first mind and decided to stay put. I wanted that nigga to taste his own blood and I was itching to make it happen.

"He's not even worth it," Duke, one of the old cats, said. He saw the looks that Troy and I exchanged.

"I already know. I'm letting him make it. I got more important shit to worry about," I replied.

"He's confused and this place is consuming him." He shook his head in pity. I wondered what he meant by that, but I didn't ask him.

"Alright, let's get this card game going. I'm ready to whip somebody's ass," I laughed.

"It's on then," Duke said while dealing the cards. The dorm was fairly quiet since most of the inmates went out on the yard.

We sat around playing cards and talking shit for a few hours. We were about to get another game started when the yard alarm started blaring. A few correction officers ran past us with their guns drawn. A few minutes later, we saw uniformed police officers, along with some members of the infirmary, running in the same direction. We were told to line up against the wall until they gave us the okay to move. It was hard for me to stay still. Quan and Lil Mike were on the yard and I needed to make sure they were alright.

"Damn man, my lil cousin and my boy are out there," I told Duke while we stood on the wall.

"Don't worry about them, they can handle themselves."

That was true. The two of them could make it through anything, but something didn't feel right about this entire situation. Every time the door opened, I tried to peek outside to see if I could see what was happening. I really started to panic when I saw two ambulance workers rushing through with a

61

gurney. I sat down on the floor to calm myself down. I said a silent prayer for Quan and Lil Mike and hoped for the best.

A few minutes later, the door flew open and they were rushing through with somebody strapped down on the gurney. I jumped up to see if I knew who it was. I had to do a double take when I saw Troy lying there unconscious. His face was swollen and covered in blood, but I still could still tell that it was him. One of his eyes was swollen shut and a huge knot rested on his forehead. It didn't take a genius to figure out that Quan and Lil Mike had gotten to him on the yard. Now I knew why they wanted me to stay inside. I was pissed that they did it without me since I was the one who really wanted him the most.

"Damn, they fucked him up. His girls gon' be mad now," Duke said, laughing. Everybody fell out when he said it, but I was confused as hell.

"What girls?" I asked, looking at him like he was crazy. The only females in here were a few busted ass correction officers.

"I'm just fucking around." He had a smirk on his face like he knew something that I didnt. I guess it was an inside joke, but I didn't plan on staying around long enough to get it. I sat back down on the floor and waited until they gave us further instructions. I felt a little better knowing that my people were most likely okay.

After waiting for over an hour, we were finally given the green light to move around the dorm again. The inmates that were outside were being let back in by the officers. I spotted Quan and Lil Mike coming through the door and made my way over to them.

"What the hell happened out there?" I asked in a low tone.

"That nigga got dealt with, plain and simple," Quan whispered back.

62

"Nigga, I hope nobody didn't see y'all. You know not to trust nobody, especially in here." Both he and Lil Mike started laughing when I said that.

"I don't see shit funny." They were starting to piss me off. I did a lot of dirt in my life, but I never got caught for most of it. That was because I did it alone and didn't tell anybody about it.

"Man, calm your nervous ass down. We didn't touch that nigga," Lil Mike said.

"Well, somebody touched his ass, judging from what I saw when he got wheeled in here," I replied.

"I didn't say nobody touched him; I said we didn't touch him. Let's just leave it at that." He walked off, letting me know that he was done talking.

"It's all good cuz. Nobody saw nothing and nobody gon' say nothing. That nigga had a lot of enemies in here, so they don't know where to start looking anyway. That's why he got transferred over here in the first place," Quan said. I really didn't give a damn that he got his ass whooped; I just didn't want them getting in trouble behind my beef.

"Man, it's whatever. I don't feel sorry for his ass. I just wish y'all would have told me what was up since I'm the one who got a problem with him. I wanted to get at him myself."

"I know you did, but there's a certain way we have to move around here. You gon' see that nigga on the streets again. Especially if he's still fucking with Keanna."

"I'm going finish my card game. You niggas need to stay out of trouble," I told him, as I walked off heading back to the table. That was easier said than done with him since trouble always seemed to follow his lead.

It was a little after one the next afternoon when one of the officers called me from the dorm for a visit. It wasn't visitation day, so I knew it had to be Mr. Gibson, my probation officer. I was kind of nervous about seeing him because I didn't know if the news he was delivering was good or bad. It was like he held my freedom in the palm of his hands and that didn't sit too well with me. I walked in the room escorted by the guard and was instructed to take a seat at the table.

"How are you, Mr. Mack?" Mr. Gibson asked while reaching his hand out to me.

"I'm good under the circumstances," I replied, shaking his hand.

"I understand and I might be able to help you out with that." I sat up straight in my chair, anticipating what he had to say. It almost sounded like he had some good news for me after all.

"I've been meaning to come see you for a while now, but I had to research some things before I came. I found a rehabilitation center in your area that I want to enroll you in."

I thought he was joking at first, but he didn't crack a smile. He really had me fucked up if he thought I was going to some damn rehab. Besides weed, I never touched drugs a day in my life unless I was selling them, and I never had to touch it then. I would do my whole two and a half years in here before I let that happen.

"Are you serious? I ain't no dope fiend. Why would I want to go to rehab?" I was getting upset and I didn't care about what I was saying.

"Just listen for a minute before you get upset," he chuckled. I didn't find a damn thing funny about him trying to send me to a "crack-be-gone" facility.

"The facility is not just for drug addiction. They offer anger management, parenting, and computer classes, as well as many other classes that I think would be beneficial to you. It's another alternative to you staying in here. The program lasts anywhere from three to six months, based on your progress."

After he explained it to me, it seemed like a good idea. I had to admit that anything sounded better than being in here.

"So, if I agree, how soon can I go?" I asked.

"Well, there is a short waiting list but, if you agree to go, I'll put you on it now. The wait is usually one month or less. The name of the facility is A New Beginning. You'll have your own room and you are allowed to bring your own clothes and a television. A phone is not allowed, but you can use the facility's phone during certain hours. You can have visitors and, occasionally, you are allowed to leave for a limited amount of time."

This was starting to sound better and better the more he spoke. I was sold.

"So, is that something you would be interested in?" he asked.

"Hell yeah!" I replied excitedly. "You can sign me up right now."

If I could leave this dungeon now, I would. Mr. Gibson laughed at my response, but I was dead ass serious.

"Good, I'm glad you accepted. Just know that you will still have to report to me for the remainder of your probation. This does not mean that you are excused from doing so," he said, standing to his feet.

"I understand. Thank you, I really appreciate everything."

"No thanks needed. Your father did most of the work. He was adamant about you not being in here. He actually recommended the facility to my supervisor and I."

Hearing that made me smile. I knew that my pops would never give up on me, no matter what the circumstances were. He told me he was looking into some things to get me out of here, but he never said what it was. I wish I didn't have to be confined at all, but at least I wouldn't have to be in here for the next two years or longer.

"Alright Mr. Mack, I'm going to make that call as soon as I get to my car. I'll be in touch with you when I have a definite date."

I stood up and shook his hand before he knocked on the door, alerting the guard of his departure. Once he left, I was escorted back to the dorm. I was sleepy before I left, but I was wide awake now. I had to keep telling myself that it was only a matter of time before I would be rolling up out of here.

"What's up fam?" Lil Mike asked when I got back to the dorm.

"Not a damn thing, what's good with you?"

"Going get in on this card game," he said, walking away while smiling.

That was where I was headed before he said that. Lil Mike was a gambler at heart, but he was also a cheater. There was no way I was getting in a card game with him playing. I made a U-turn and headed to the phone banks. My pops really came through for me and I wanted to call and tell him how much I appreciated it.

My brother, Eric, was making sure that my businesses were running smooth too. He used the money that came from that to make sure the bills were paid and my kids were straight. I had a lot of unfinished business to take care of, starting with getting a divorce from Cherika's crazy ass. And I was definitely getting a paternity test once she dropped her load. I was sure she thought that having a baby would change my mind, but she was in for a rude awakening. We were through and there was no coming back.

I also wanted to see what was up with Alexus. If she thought I was going away just like that, she had another thing coming. I wanted her to look me in the eyes and tell me that it was over instead of running like she always did. The possibility of seeing her again made me smile. I just hoped she felt the same way.

Chapter 7

I was so happy to be done with my last exam. I had three classes and all three professors gave tests on the same day. I was overwhelmed and exhausted from studying day and night, but it paid off. I made an A on each one of them and I was ready to celebrate. Jada, the twins, and I were meeting up at the hibachi bar and grill to have drinks and catch up. Actually, Jada was the only one we needed to catch up with because the twins and I were always together. She finally decided to come up for air and spend some time with us. I was so happy when she called me, but I still had a few bones to pick with her.

After I spent some time with my girls, I wanted to go see Tyree. I really needed to do something special for him. We hadn't seen each other in two days because of me studying day and night. I stayed at my mama's house so I wouldn't be distracted by him and he was not too happy about it. I sent him a text telling him that I would be over as soon as I left the restaurant. I had my duffle bag packed with a few surprises I was sure he would like.

I pulled up to the restaurant, but I didn't see anybody else's car. I decided to sit in my car and wait until someone else arrived. I pulled up my Facebook page on my phone and scrolled through my timeline. I jumped when I heard a knock on the passenger side window. I looked to see who it was before rolling the window down.

"Girl, you scared the hell out of me," I said, holding my chest.

"Sorry. What are you doing out here by yourself?" Keanna asked me.

"I'm waiting for Jada and my sisters-in-law to get here. After all those exams I took today, I need a drink."

I was hoping that she was meeting someone else here so she didn't ask to join us. Jada would have a fit if she showed up and Keanna was there.

"I hear that girl. I'm just coming to get take out. I just left the gym so I'm not dressed to stay."

I never noticed the leggings and tennis shoes she wore, but I was happy to hear that she was leaving.

"Okay, well, I'll see you later."

"Alright girl, have fun," Keanna said before going into the restaurant. I rolled the window up and got out of the car. I was about to call Jada, but she was already pulling up. She was a few minutes late, but at least she showed up this time. When she got out of the car, she ran over and gave me a big hug.

"Hey friend, I missed you," she squealed, squeezing the life out of me. I hugged her back because I genuinely missed her too.

"I missed you too, but I'm still pissed with you," I said, pulling away from her.

"I know and I'm truly sorry for shutting you out. I have a lot going on with me right now, but I promise we'll talk about everything soon. You just have to promise not to hate me afterwards."

"Hate you? Why would I hate you? You know that would never happen." I looked at her in confusion. She wasn't making any sense to me.

"Yeah, you say that now. I just really don't think you'll understand."

"Well, try me," I snapped. She was pissing me off. If we were best friends like she said we were, then she should know that she could talk to me about anything.

"I'm listening," I said with my hand on my hips.

"Ugh, look at this bitch," she whispered, looking behind me. I turned around and saw Keanna walking up with food in her hands.

"Hey Jada," she said with a smirk on her face.

"Girl bye," Jada said, walking off.

"That's your bestie," Keanna said, laughing.

"What's up with y'all?" I asked. "We all used to get along just fine a few years ago. As a matter of fact, y'all were friends before I even came into the picture."

I knew that Jada was pissed with Keanna for hooking me up with Dre, but this was ridiculous. It seemed to be more personal than that.

"Exactly, but you need to ask her that question. I'm not the one with the problem," Keanna said, walking off. I didn't know what was going on and nobody seemed to want to tell me anything. I made my way up the stairs to the patio and sat down next to Jada.

"Trina said that they're on their way," Jada said once I sat down.

"That's cool, but we need to talk." I looked at her letting her know just how serious I was.

"Can we please not do this right now Lex? I'm really not in the mood."

"I really don't care about what mood you're in. Something is up with you and you need to start talking. I'm tired of doing the back and forth thing, and I'm tired of you talking in riddles," I snapped. She looked at me with watery eyes and grabbed my hand.

"Ok, but you have to promise me that nothing will change between us. You're my best friend and I already feel like I'm ruining our friendship by keeping secrets," she cried. I grabbed a tissue from my purse and wiped her eyes.

"What's wrong Jada? You're scaring me." I was nervous and her tears weren't helping the situation. I just prayed that it wasn't anything serious. It couldn't have been health related because I'm sure she wouldn't have kept that from me. She leaned her head on my shoulder and cried while I tried my best to comfort her.

"Girl, look at these dyke bitches," I heard, followed by laughter. I looked up and saw that hood rat, Cherika, and her nasty ass sister, Charde, standing there watching us. Jada sat up and wiped her eyes and looked over at both of them. She was done crying. I could tell that she was alert and ready for whatever.

"I can't be too much of a dyke, just ask your husband," I said, laughing along with Jada. She stopped laughing when I said that. I knew I hit a nerve, so I kept going.

"When does my boo come home anyway?" I asked, messing with her. She took a step towards me, but her sister pulled her back.

"You're not stupid; you know what an ass whooping from me feels like." I stood to my feet, preparing to issue another one if I had to.

"Bitch, don't flatter yourself. I'm just not trying to lose my baby fighting with your dumb ass," she said, rubbing her belly. I had to do a double take when I saw the small pouch that she was rubbing. She looked like she gained some weight, so it was possible that she was pregnant.

"Girl, that ain't nothing but a beer belly. The same one that you've been having forever. The same one that your husband hated." I smiled knowing that I was getting to her.

"Obviously, he didn't hate it too much or I wouldn't be having another one of his babies," she said matter-of-factly. I hadn't seen or talked to Dre in months but, for some reason, her comment pissed me off, even though I would never show it. I shouldn't have been surprised, but I was. After all, she was his wife. I could tell that she wanted to play dirty and I was more than prepared.

"I hope you're sure that it's his this time. I would hate to have a repeat of what happened with Drew," I smirked.

"Oh, no doubt about it, he is definitely the father. Every time he left your bed, he climbed right back into mine." She was the one smirking this time.

"Was that before or after he asked for a divorce?" I countered. She wasn't laughing after that.

"Fuck you, Alexus!" she yelled.

"I'll pass but, when Dre comes home, tell him that he can most definitely get it," I said, walking away.

Cherika was still yelling and cursing, but I kept going without looking back. Jada followed me through the restaurant and into the bathroom. I grabbed a hand full of paper towels and wet them with cold water. As hard as I tried, I couldn't stop the tears from flowing. I shouldn't have been hurt, but I was and I really didn't know why. Dre should have been the

73

last person on my mind but, thanks to Cherika, he was all that I could think of at the moment.

"What the hell are you crying for?" Jada asked while wiping my face.

"I don't know." I sobbed into the paper towels that I was holding.

"Are you serious right now Alexus? You have a damn good man and you in here crying behind Dre's dog ass?" Jada was looking at me like I was crazy and maybe I was.

"I know, I'm good now," I said, wiping my eyes. I didn't know what came over me, but it was gone just as fast as it came.

"You better be good because Trina just sent me a text saying that they're outside. How did we go from me crying on your shoulder to you crying on mine?" Jada laughed.

I laughed too as she helped me wipe my face and pull myself together. I applied some gloss to my lips and checked myself in the mirror before we exited the bathroom. I couldn't let Tyree's sisters see that I had been crying. They would tell him and that would open another can of worms that I wasn't prepared for.

"Hey y'all," Tina said as we met them outside.

"Give me a hug stranger," Trina said to Jada. Just like me, they hadn't seen her in a while.

"Please don't start trying to make me feel bad. I feel bad enough as it is," Jada said, hugging both of her cousins.

"You should feel bad, but I'm hungry; let's go find somewhere to sit," Tina said, holding her stomach. We found a table right next to the bar and that was perfect for me. I needed a drink in the worst way. Jada stopped a passing waitress and we all placed our drink and food orders.

"So, what's been going on with you cousin?" Trina asked. She was usually the more outspoken one out of the two sisters.

"Nothing much," Jada said, shrugging her shoulders.

"Well, something must be going on. Nobody has been seeing you and we barely talk to you. This new man must really be the shit. From what I heard, he got you babysitting and everything," Trina said all in one breath.

"Babysitting! I know this nigga don't have you watching his damn kids!" I yelled, looking at Jada in surprise. This was news to me. Jada loved kids, but I'd never known her to babysit for anyone. As much as I loved Dre and his kids, I never kept them when he wasn't around.

"It's not even like that. That was something that I chose to do. And you have a very big mouth by the way," Jada said, rolling her eyes at Tina.

"I didn't know it was a secret," Tina replied nonchalantly. So, she was talking to Tina about her mystery man, but she couldn't talk to me. This was not the Jada that I knew and loved. Something was going on with her and I couldn't wait to find out what it was. I kept replaying the conversation we had earlier over and over in my head. Why would she think I would hate her? She was close to telling me before Cherika interrupted us, but I knew that she wouldn't say anything as long as her cousins were around.

"So, when can we meet him?" Trina asked, breaking me from my thoughts. That was the million-dollar question that everyone wanted the answer to.

"I don't know Trina," Jada said, sounding uncomfortable.

"Is he ugly or something?" I asked. I figured that maybe she was ashamed of him or something.

"No," Jada said, laughing.

"Well, what is it?" Tina asked.

"Can we just enjoy our time together without talking about my love life?" Jada asked us. We all nodded our heads, agreeing to drop it for now. I had more questions, but I didn't want to ask them in front of everyone. I pulled out my phone and sent Jada a text telling her that we needed to set aside a time to talk, just the two of us. When she read the text, she looked up at me and nodded. I would let her make it for now, but this conversation was far from being over. We enjoyed our food and drinks as well as each other's company for the rest of the night.

Chapter 8

66 "That bitch was sick when I told her that I was pregnant. Did you see her face?" I said excitedly to my sister, Charde.

"She didn't look like she cared to me," Charde replied with a shrug.

"Oh, she was definitely in her feelings."

I laughed as I thought back to our entire encounter. She tried to play it off, but I could see the hurt all in Alexus' face. I didn't understand how she could possibly be upset about me having a baby with my own damn husband. I was happy that she could finally feel some of the pain that she and Dre inflicted on me. She may have moved on, but she still had feelings for Dre and that much was obvious.

I couldn't lie though; some of her comments hit below the belt, mostly because they were true. There was no denying that Dre was in love with her at one point. I just hoped that their time apart was long enough for him to see that it was really over between them.

"Bring me to the store before you drop me off home. I want some ice cream," I told Charde.

She gave me the side eye and I just knew something slick was about to come out of her mouth.

"Bitch, you're already getting fat as fuck. You keep on and Dre and nobody else will want you."

"Bitch, I'm pregnant. You act like I'm gaining weight just because. And Dre ain't going nowhere, please believe that."

"Whatever, I know you saw how that youngster had his ass gone before. Don't think for a second that her pretty face and nice shape ain't have nothing to do with it. Having his babies ain't enough no more. You better step your game up."

She was forever saying something stupid and I was sick of hearing her mouth. She should have been happy that I was even speaking to her ass after the shit that she pulled with Dre a few months ago.

"You know what? Just bring me home and I'll get my own car and go where I need to go myself," I said with much attitude.

We rode in silence for the duration of the trip. I really felt some kind of way about her trying to put me down for Alexus. It's like she wanted Dre to be with somebody else. I always knew that she was a hater so that didn't surprise me one bit. I got out of her car and slammed the door behind me without uttering so much as a goodbye.

Chapter 9

Tonight had to be my lucky night. After my run-in with Alexus and Jada at the restaurant, I got in my car and was prepared to head home. My intentions were to get me something to eat and go in for the rest of the night. I spent over 2 hours at the gym, and I was tired and hungry. I was backing out of my parking space when I spotted what appeared to be Cherika and her sister, Charde, coming out of the restaurant. I put my car in park and sat there for a few seconds, just to make sure it really was them.

My suspicions were confirmed when I saw them stop near Alexus and Jada. They appeared to be arguing about something, but I couldn't hear what they were saying. All the tiredness I felt a minute ago was quickly replaced by a huge burst of energy. My adrenaline was pumping and I was ready for war. The memories of the night they jumped me outside the daiquiri shop came rushing back to my mind. Even if I never got at her sisters, Cherika had to be dealt with. She had crossed me too many times. I still wasn't over her having a baby with Troy and I never would be.

I watched as her and Charde made their way over to a Honda Civic to the far left of the parking lot and got in. They pulled out of their parking spot and I waited for a few seconds before I pulled out right behind them. I made sure to stay a few cars behind so I wouldn't be seen. They appeared to be deep in conversation so they probably wouldn't have noticed me anyway. I could tell that they were headed to Cherika's house, judging by the way they were going. I didn't know if she was being dropped off or if her sister was staying so I kept following them to see.

I followed them for another 10 minutes until they turned on Cherika's street. I waited before turning to avoid being seen. After I felt that I waited long enough, I turned the corner just in time to see Cherika hop out of her sister's car. Charde didn't park, so I knew that she was leaving and I couldn't have been happier. My plan was to jump out of the car on Cherika before she had a chance to make it inside, but that never happened. When she got out of Charde's car, she hopped right into hers. I had no idea where she was going and I was almost prepared to give up on my mission. I pulled up behind a car that was parked two doors down from her house and killed my lights. She sat in her car for a while, as if she was contemplating her next move.

Finally, after waiting for about five more minutes, she started the car up and started backing out of her driveway. This time, I didn't wait before pulling out right behind her. I followed her out of the subdivision and onto the main highway. We drove a few more blocks before she pulled up to a small convenience store.

This was perfect. The area wasn't very well lit and there was no one out here to witness the ass whooping that I was about to deliver. It was even better that I was dressed for the occasion with my leggings and tennis shoes that I wore to the gym. She was even stupid enough to park her car on the side of the building, instead of the front where there were plenty of spaces. She was making this too easy for me.

As soon as she opened her car door, I opened mine and jumped out. She started walking towards the entrance, but she didn't get very far before I approached her from behind. I could have hit her without her even knowing it, but that would have defeated the purpose. I wasn't a coward, so I wanted her to see my face when I threw my first punch.

"What's up with it Cherika?" I yelled as I jumped in front of her. She grabbed her chest and stopped walking when she saw that it was me. The look of fear in her eyes was a welcomed surprise for me since she always had something smart to say. Cherika couldn't fight worth a damn, but she had a mouth piece that made you think otherwise. Even if she was scared, you would never know it by the way she popped off. Her smart mouth was one of the many reasons why she stayed getting into fights. She lost most of them, but that never stopped her.

"What's up with what?" she said, looking like a lost child.

"Don't act like you don't know what the deal is. You don't think I forgot about you and your scary ass sisters jumping me, huh?" I asked with my hands on my hips. She wasn't stupid, so she knew exactly what this was about.

"Look, I'm pregnant, so I'm not about to risk losing my baby to fight you. Once I drop this load, I'll be happy to give you a round or two." She clutched her belly for emphasis.

I looked down at her stomach and noticed the small bulge, but I wasn't convinced that she was pregnant. Cherika was a known beer drinker, so her stomach had been big for months. I hadn't talked to my family in a while, so I didn't know if it was true or not. Eric never mentioned her being pregnant. Honestly, I didn't care if she was pregnant. She should have thought about all of that before her and her sisters jumped me.

"I'm not about to sit out here all night entertaining you and your bullshit," she said while trying to walk past me. That was a mistake in itself. Her mouth was forever getting her in trouble, but she never learned.

"You don't have to wait all night; this won't take long," I said as I punched her in her face.

The first lick seemed to daze her momentarily, but it didn't stop her from swinging back. We went toe to toe for a little while, and I was shocked at how well she was keeping up with me. I guess at some point she got tired of getting her ass whooped all the time because she was swinging like her life depended on it. There was no way I was letting this hoe get the best of me if I could help it.

"Hey, break it up!" a male voice yelled before pulling Cherika and I apart. Once I came up for air, I saw that it was the young clerk who cleaned up and restocked the store who had intervened. He was no more than sixteen or seventeen years old, so I didn't care about anything that he was saying.

"Y'all better leave before somebody calls the police," he said, looking at both of us. Cherika was leaned up against her car, trying to catch her breath. I backed up, but I had no intentions of leaving. This fight was far from over.

"Get in your car and leave Miss," he said, looking at me.

"Fuck you, lil boy!" I yelled back. I was pissed that he broke us up.

"Alright, I'll just let the police deal with it. I'm going call them and I hope your ghetto ass go to jail."

He walked off and I was happy to see him go. I really didn't give a damn about him, but I wasn't trying to go to jail. Going home was about the only option I had at this point. I picked my keys up off the ground and turned to walk back to my car.

"Tell my baby daddy I said hello," Cherika laughed as I walked away.

All she had to do was keep her mouth shut, but she couldn't even do that. I thought back on everything that took place in my life over the last few years. Besides Troy, Cherika had been the source of a lot of the pain and hurt that I felt, and for her to rub it in was the last straw. I refused to walk away from this fight with her still standing.

I turned back around and ran full force at her. She was preparing to swing, but I had something else in mind. I lifted my leg and kicked her with all the strength I had. The kick was so powerful; it sent us both flying to the ground. Unlike Cherika, I was back on my feet in no time, while she laid there squirming on the ground. I didn't stop with one kick; I kicked her repeatedly in her face and all over her body until my legs gave out on me. I kneeled beside her and delivered a series of punches all over her body, while she tried to cover her face. My hands starting aching and that was the only thing that stopped me from beating Cherika to death in that parking lot.

"I hate you!" I screamed as I lifted myself up from the ground.

I really did hate her for betraying me the way she did. Before she started sleeping with Troy, Cherika and I had a very close relationship. When Dre first started doing her wrong, I was the first one to call him out on it. After she did me wrong, I was so hurt; I started helping him dog her ass out. I looked up and saw the store clerk and the manager rushing towards the entrance where we were. The manager had the phone to his ear, so it was obvious that he was calling the cops. I was no fool, so I did what came naturally. I ran to my car as fast as I could and hopped in. I didn't want them to get my license plate number, so I backed out of the parking lot and quickly sped away. I looked out of my rearview mirror and saw the men trying to lift Cherika's bloodied body from the ground. She would think twice before crossing me again and that much I was sure of.

Chapter 10

"Everything is going to be alright, an ambulance is on the way," Mr. Milton, the store's manager, said while wiping my face with a warm towel.

My entire body was in excruciating pain. I knew my right eye was swollen because I could barely see out of it. The front of my cream-colored shirt was covered in blood. Mr. Milton and the store clerk tried to help me up from the ground, but I was in too much pain to move. I wanted to call somebody, but I didn't know where my phone or my purse was. The only thing I could do right now was pray. I especially prayed for the health of my unborn baby. I would be devastated if I lost this baby.

This pregnancy was my last attempt at winning my husband back. As cold hearted as Dre was, he had a soft spot for his kids, so he wouldn't leave me while I was pregnant. Well, that was what I was hoping for anyway. I couldn't believe Keanna did this to me even after I told her that I was pregnant. She was salty about what happened between me and Troy. I didn't blame her, but she could have waited until after my baby was born.

"Who was that lady you were fighting with?" Mr. Milton asked, kneeling next to me. As much as I hated her and wanted her to go down, snitching was not something that I could do. Kenna would be dealt with in a different way. If she thought my sisters and I beat her down before, that was nothing compared to what was coming.

"I don't know," I lied. "She hit me from behind, so I didn't see her face." They couldn't prove if I was telling the truth or not so they had to take my word.

"We couldn't get her plate number because she backed out of the parking lot," he said, shaking his head.

"Can someone call my sister and let her know what's going on?" I asked in a raspy voice. I wanted to call Cherice. Charde was the last person that I wanted to see right now.

"Okay, we have your phone and purse. I'll bring it to you so you can call someone," Mr. Milton said, walking away. I heard the sirens in the distance and I was relieved that help was on the way. With a few bandages, I would be fine, but I needed to know if my baby was alright.

"Here you go," Mr. Milton said, handing me my phone.

"Can you dial my sister's number for me, please?"

After dialing the number I gave him, he handed me the phone just as the ambulance was pulling up.

"Hello," Cherice answered on the second ring.

"I'm about to go to the hospital," I said into the receiver.

"Cherika?!" she asked loudly, verifying who I was.

"Yeah, it's me."

"What happened, why are you going to the hospital?" Cherice was always the calm one, but even she sounded nervous right now. Before I had a chance to answer, the paramedics were rushing over to assist me.

"She got attacked by some woman in the parking lot," Mr. Milton told them. One of the female paramedics came over with a first aid kit and started applying some type of ointment to my wounds.

"We're going to need to bring you in to see a doctor. You have a few deep cuts that may require some attention," the paramedic told me.

"I'm pregnant; I need to have my baby checked out," I told her while holding my stomach.

"Oh God. How far along are you?"

"I'm four months today."

"Okay, let's get you to the hospital. We need the gurney!" she yelled to her male co-worker.

"Cherika!" Cherice yelled through the phone. I had completely forgotten about her and she was going crazy.

"What hospital are we going to?" I asked. "I want my sister to meet me there."

"West Jefferson is the closest, so we'll be going there," she replied. I relayed the information to my sister and hung up the phone.

"Can you stand?" the male paramedic asked me. I was still in a lot of pain, so I shook my head saying no.

"Okay, I'm going to lift you on the count of three," he said, standing over me. After counting to three, he lifted me up, and I instantly knew that something was wrong.

"Ahhh!" I screamed to the top of my lungs. I felt the warm liquid between my legs, but I was too scared to look down. The bottom of my stomach starting cramping and I knew that wasn't a good sign.

"Oh God, please don't let this be happening to me," I cried out in pain.

The paramedics put me in the back of their truck and rushed me away from the scene. The blaring sirens made me feel more uncomfortable because I knew that this was indeed an emergency. I was so scared and being alone didn't help the situation. As much as my mama aggravated me sometimes, I would give anything if she were here to comfort me right now. Maybe I should have called her before calling my sister. Her answer to everything was prayer and that was something that I needed lots of right now.

"Please hurry, I think I might be losing my baby," I cried. It felt like this ride was taking forever.

"We're almost there ma'am," the paramedic responded. And just as she promised, we were pulling up to the emergency entrance within the next two minutes. Both paramedics rushed to the back of the truck and pulled me out. Once they wheeled me in, they informed the doctors of what was going on with me.

"What's your name dear?" one of the doctors asked me.

"Cherika Mack," I responded.

"Okay Cherika, I'm Dr. Lee. We're going to bring you to labor and delivery to see what going on with the little one," he said while holding my hand.

Dr. Lee was a short, bald-headed Asian man, but his voice was very comforting to me. I nodded my head in response and we were on our way. When we got to labor and delivery, two orderlies were told to move me from the gurney to the hospital bed. Once they moved me, I looked over to the gurney that I came in on and almost lost my mind. I screamed as I saw the dark red blood that stained most of the once white sheets and from the pains that were shooting throughout my entire body.

"It's okay sweetheart, we're going to give you something for the pain," Dr. Lee said. He called a nurse in to remove my clothes and start an I.V. on me. She ended up cutting my pants off, but it didn't matter since they were already ruined by all the blood.

"How far along were you?" she asked me when she was done.

Maybe she didn't realize it, but she had just confirmed the loss of my baby with one little word: were. All hope was lost for me. I felt like I was having an out of body experience and everything was moving in slow motion. My baby didn't survive and there was nothing that I could do about it. Dr. Lee was saying something to the nurse, but I didn't hear one word that he said. A little while later, my eyelids started getting heavy, so I knew I must have been given something to help me relax. With any luck, I would go to sleep and never wake up.

Chapter 11

"Bring me a bottle of water baby!" I yelled to Alexus as she walked to the kitchen.

She had been at my house for the past week and that was all good with me. Before then, she was staying at her mama's house to study for her exams. We had just come back in from doing a 3-mile run and I was exhausted.

For the past few days, all my exercise came from the bedroom only since Alexus and I had to make up for lost time. She more than made up for her absence when she showed up with a grab bag full of treats last week. She brought everything from whipped cream to edible underwear and we used it all. I was determined to make her stay here as long as possible this time around.

"Here you go," Alexus said, handing me a bottle of

water.

"I'm going take a shower," she announced while attempting to walk away.

"Wait, let me talk to you for a minute."

She came and sat down next to me on the sofa and turned on the tv. Something was bothering me and I wanted to talk to her about it. I wasn't the type to keep my feelings to myself, so I put it out there.

"Why didn't you tell me that Keanna and your ex are cousins?" I asked her. She looked away before answering me. I was sure she was wondering how I found out since she didn't bother telling me.

"I didn't think it was that important."

"That's not the point. When I asked you how you knew her, you should have said something then. You're making me think you have something to hide," I said, looking at her.

"I don't have anything to hide. I told you everything that you wanted to know."

"No, you told me everything that you wanted me to know."

She looked like I hurt her feelings, but I had to speak my mind. I was always taught to never keep my feelings bottled up because it only made matters worse. I pulled her onto my lap and hugged her around her waist as I spoke.

"I'm not trying to hurt your feelings baby, but I need us to be open and honest with each other. I don't keep anything from you and I don't want you to start hiding stuff from me."

Alexus was someone that I wanted to build a future with, but we couldn't build anything based on lies.

"I know and I'm sorry, but I wasn't trying to hide it from you. Dre is my past and I don't want him nowhere in my future," she said, looking at me. I understood that because I felt the same way about a few people in my life, and Mikayla was one of them.

"I understand. As long as we're on the same page, I'm cool," I said, kissing her lips.

"We're on the same page," she replied, standing to her feet. She headed for the stairs but stopped before she went up.

"Who told you that Dre and Keanna were cousins?"

I knew that was coming. After the speech that I just gave her, I didn't have a choice other than to tell the truth.

"Keanna told me." Damn. I hated to rat ole girl out, but I really didn't have a choice.

"I thought so," she replied, frowning.

"Wait," I said, standing to my feet. I didn't need her to be involved with no foolishness with Keanna. It really wasn't that serious.

"Leave that shit alone Lex. She thought I already knew. That's the only reason why she mentioned it."

She put her hand on her hip and looked at me like I was crazy.

"You are not blind and you're far from stupid. Her ass told you that because she is messy. I don't even know why I'm surprised. She keeps up bullshit in her own family, so I know that I'm nobody special. She's feeling you and everybody can see it but you."

I could tell that Keanna had a lil crush on me, but that was as far as it would go. She wasn't my type at all.

"I can't wait to see her messy ass," she said before stomping up the stairs.

Alexus was the sweetest person in the world until somebody pissed her off. I finished my bottle of water and turned off the tv before going upstairs behind her.

"You are too pretty to be out there with all that fighting and stuff. Not to mention, that shit is childish," I said when I walked into the bedroom.

"Who said anything about fighting? I just said I can't wait to see her." She replied with a sneaky smirk on her face. I knew that look well enough to know that this was far from over.

"Are you getting in the shower with me?" she asked, smiling.

"Don't try to change the subject." I looked at her as she started undressing. Keanna and nobody else were on my mind right now. That body was enough to make me forget about everything and everybody.

"That's cool, I can shower by myself," she said as she walked into the master bathroom naked.

I damn sure wasn't about to let that happen. I started taking my clothes off as fast as I could to join her. This was why I hated it when she left. I was walking towards the bathroom when my phone started ringing. I almost ignored it, but I didn't. Me and my pops had been bidding on a few properties and I didn't want to miss any calls. I had to do a double take when I saw Mikayla's number show up. It wasn't saved in my phone anymore, but I still recognized it. I had no idea what she wanted, but I was damn sure going to find out. Alexus would have a fit if she knew Kayla was calling my phone. I heard the shower turn on and I was happy for the distraction. The running water was loud enough to drown out the sound of my ringing phone.

"Hello," I said in a whisper.

"Hey Ty, how you doing?" she asked like it was cool for her to be calling me.

"I'm good Kayla, but what you want?" I didn't mean to be rude, but she was crossing the line.

"Oh, um, my mama wanted me to call you about some property. She's thinking about expanding her business and she's looking for a bigger place."

I was happy to hear that she was calling about business, but it still wasn't a good look for her to be calling me on my personal phone. I had a business line that she was more than welcomed to call. As a matter of fact, it might be best for her and her family to deal with my pops. I didn't want or need no more drama between me and Alexus.

"That's cool but let me give you my daddy's number. He can talk to you about what we have available." I was trying my best to rush her off the phone.

"I just called him and he told me to call you." She laughed but that shit wasn't funny to me.

Damn! I thought to myself. I made a mental note to ask him about that shit. He knew her crazy ass was the last person that I would want to do business with.

"Alright but, next time, you need to call on my business line. I have a girl and I don't want any drama with you calling on my personal line."

"Oh, I'm sorry. I'm not trying to cause any trouble for y'all. I'll make sure to call your other phone from now on."

"Cool, tell your mama that I'll get in touch with her sometime tomorrow. We can talk more about it then," I said before hanging up. I erased her number and prepared to take a shower with my baby. I wasn't trying to hide anything, but I didn't know how I was going to handle the situation. No matter what I said, Alexus was not going to be cool with me working with Mikayla. At the same time, I couldn't turn away a potential client. I just went in on her about keeping things from me and here I was doing the exact same thing. I made my way to the shower and forgot about it for the time being. I just hoped my decision didn't come back to bite me in the ass later.

Chapter 12

Two weeks later and it was official. I was accepted into the New Beginning program and I would be heading over there tomorrow. That was the best news that I'd heard all day. According to Mr. Gibson, they had a very long waiting list, so I might not have to stay in there as long as I thought. It really didn't matter to me either way. Doing six months in a rehab facility was better than doing two and a half years in prison.

"Pass the ball nigga!" Quan yelled to me from across the yard. We were outside playing basketball and I was standing there daydreaming in the middle of the game.

"My bad, I'm thinking about tomorrow," I said, passing him the ball.

"That's what's up. I'm happy that you're getting the

hell up out of here."

I was more than happy. The sooner I started the program, the sooner I would be able to get home. I talked to my brother earlier, and he and my sister had my clothes packed already. He told me that they purchased all my hygiene items and everything would be waiting for me when I got there. The facility was only about a twenty-minute drive from my condo, so that was perfect.

"There they go," Lil Mike said, walking over to us.

He was referring to a group of men who were walking in our direction. There was an area on the yard that I was told to never go into when I first arrived. I never asked why, but I never went over there either. The area was hidden by an old iron door that blocked off the people who frequented the area. I saw Troy go back there a few times, so I knew that it couldn't have been good.

"What the hell do they be doing back there?" I asked Quan and Lil Mike.

"Everything," Quan replied like it was nothing.

"Man, anything goes in the cut," Mike said.

"If you want to get high, get some head, or anything else, that's the place to be." I looked at him like he was crazy. I wasn't green to doing time, but this was like being in another world. I never saw a prison that let the prisoners run the show like this.

"So, them niggas are back there getting their dicks sucked by another man, while the rest of them are standing there watching like that?" I asked, laughing.

"Yep, and ole boy be on that foul shit right along with them," Mike replied.

As if on cue, Troy came walking out on the yard and headed straight for the danger zone with two other dudes following right behind him. He was released from the hospital last week, but that didn't stop him from falling back into his old habits.

"Man, I know his stupid ass ain't in here playing with no lil boys," I said in shock. During the entire time I ran with Troy, I would have never suspected him of being a switch hitter. He had just as many side chicks as me most of the time. At one point, I assumed he was on dope, but this was a whole new game that he was playing.

"What? He's the ring leader. Why do you think he got moved from the other dorm? He was fighting every other day and fucking every other night," Mike said as he and Quan fell out laughing. I thought back to the comment that Duke made a few weeks ago about 'his girls' being mad when he got beat up, and it all made sense to me now.

"That nigga gay?" I asked the question more to myself.

"I guess he go both ways, since he like girls too," Quan said.

"That's fucked up. Keanna don't even know who she's sleeping with." It was fucked up for me too since we ran in the same circle for years and I didn't even know. Honestly, I didn't feel bad for Keanna at all. She was so busy minding everybody else's business; she was blind to what was going on under her own roof.

I no longer had a desire to play ball, so I sat down and watched as everybody else ran up and down the yard doing their thing. It was like nobody was who I thought they were. Troy was an undercover homo. Alexus straight up abandoned me when I was at my lowest point. Keanna was so sneaky; I didn't know what she was capable of anymore. The list of people that I trusted was getting shorter and shorter by the minute.

I didn't even know where to start with Cherika. I hadn't heard from her since she came to visit me a while ago. This whole pregnancy thing had me feeling some kind of way. I didn't want her no more, so having more kids with her was the last thing that I wanted to do.

My sister Erica was trying to tell me something about her being in the hospital, but I cut her off before she could finish talking. I made it crystal clear to her that if it wasn't about my kids, I didn't want to hear anything about Cherika. If I was proven to be the new baby's father, I would handle my business with this one just like I did with the others.

"Look at this clown," Quan said, breaking me from my thoughts.

I looked up and saw Troy coming from behind the iron door, followed by the same two dudes that he went back there with. His belt was undone and he was fixing his pants while he walked. That was enough confirmation for me to know that something wasn't right with him. He looked up at me and I smirked at him while shaking my head in disgust. He quickly looked away and kept walking towards the other side of the yard. The look of guilt and shame on his face was not to be mistaken.

"I told you that he was foul," Lil Mike said while dribbling the ball between his legs.

"You learn something new every day," I said, standing to my feet. That was one saying that was very true.

The next morning, I woke up before the guards had a chance to get me up. I was full of anxiety and I couldn't stay still for more than a minute. It was so bad that I started making everybody else around me nervous.

"Man, sit your crazy ass down somewhere! It's not even time for you to go yet," Quan yelled from his bunk.

Mr. Gibson was coming to sign me out and transport me to the facility at nine, but it wasn't even six o'clock yet. I didn't give a damn what Quan was talking about; I was ready to bounce. Usually, I would talk to Duke when I was up this early, but even he was still sleeping. I was pacing back and forth like a caged animal. The only difference was I was prepared to be set free, ready to get back to the money.

I heard keys jingling and I knew that the guards were on their way to do the morning count. That meant that it was six o'clock and I only had three hours left.

"I'm glad your nervous ass is leaving. You're getting on my damn nerves with all this pacing and shit," Quan said as he came and stood next to me.

"Nigga, shut up. I bet you feel the same way when it's time for you to go," I replied.

I didn't know how long Quan had been in here, but he had six more months to go before he was released. I made sure I wrote down him and Lil Mike's info, so I could make sure they were straight once I was home. Four guards walked down the hall and started the process of making sure that all the prisoners were accounted for. Once they completed that, we could eat or do whatever until it was time for them to count again. That seemed like the only time a guard was around.

For me, eating was out of the question because I didn't have an appetite. I never ate the food that was served in here anyway, so I made sure to keep my commissary stacked. Since I was leaving today, I divided everything I had between Quan, Lil Mike, and Duke. I used up all the remaining money in my account to buy more stuff for them to have after I was gone.

"You gon' get at Lex when you get out?" Quan asked me. That was a question that was hard for me to answer. A part of me was still in love with her and I couldn't figure out why. She basically threw up her middle finger to me the minute I got locked up. Actually, she threw it up way before I got locked up. She was creepin' right up under my nose and I didn't even know it. But, at the same time, we had a lot of unresolved issues that I wanted to get to the bottom of. Alexus was the worst kind of cheater because you would never suspect her of doing anything wrong. She was sneaky as hell and that was really the only problem I had with her.

"I don't know, man. It's like I want to but then, I don't. What do you think I should do?" I asked. I was a grown ass man, so it really didn't matter to me what anyone else thought, but I was curious about his opinion.

"To be honest with you, cousin, shorty bad as hell, but I wouldn't fuck with her no more. She was down bad for doing you wrong like that."

As much as I wanted to, I couldn't even get mad. I asked for his opinion and he gave it to me. As much as I hated to admit it, he was right. I put her wants and needs before my own wife's and look at where it got me. As ghetto and ratchet as Cherika was, she always had my back no matter what. Before I met Alexus, I wouldn't have dreamed of asking her for a divorce for that reason alone.

"I know Cherika did some foul shit, but maybe you need to rethink that divorce," Quan said, breaking me from my thoughts.

"Sometimes, I feel like I should think on it some more but, at the same time, I really don't want to be married no more. I'm not cut out for that shit."

It wasn't fair for me to stay married to Cherika when I knew that I could never be faithful to her. Even before Alexus came along, I cheated so many times; I lost count.

102

"You might be right about that. You can't be with just one broad." Quan laughed but it was true.

"Yes, I can. If it's the one that I want."

"I know you're talking about Alexus. You're going back to her; I can tell by the way you're talking."

"I don't know, but I'm not gon' lie and say that I ain't gon' try." As stupid as I know I sounded, I was honest about my feelings. The heart couldn't help who or what it fell in love with. There no was denying that Alexus still had my heart.

"Mack, let's go!" the guard yelled when he opened the cell. It was only eight thirty, but that was music to my ears. I jumped up and made my way over to him. I had already said my goodbyes, so I was ready to roll.

"Keep in touch fam!" Quan yelled to me as I made my exit. I followed the guard down the hall with extra pep in my step. As soon as we made it through the doors, I spotted Mr. Gibson in the visitation room.

"Good morning Mr. Mack. How are you feeling today?" he asked.

I was feeling good like a muthafucka, but I couldn't tell that to him.

"I'm doing good sir," was my simple reply.

"I know that I'm a little early, but your brother dropped off some clothes for you to change into. Let me see if I can find a place for you to change." He was about to walk off when I stopped him.

"Hold up, you don't have to find nowhere for me to change. We're all men; I can change right here," I said in a hurry. There was no sense in prolonging my stay here. I grabbed the bag that held my clothes and started stripping out of the dirty jumper and underclothes that the jailhouse provided for me. I had been showering with other niggas for months so that was nothing.

Mr. Gibson and the guard started laughing, as I stood there butt ass naked for the whole world to see. I didn't give a damn. I put my fresh clothes on and handed the guard what belonged to them.

"I'm ready," I said, turning to face Mr. Gibson.

"I can see that," he replied, smiling.

After he stopped at the front desk and filled out the necessary paperwork for my release, we were on our way. I hadn't been gone that long, but it felt damn good to be on the outside again. It felt even better to be in my own clothes. The only thing that I was missing was a fresh haircut. I was probably pushing my luck, but I was about to ask Mr. Gibson for another favor.

"What time am I supposed to be at the facility?" I asked, looking over at him.

"Check-in time is before noon. I came early just in case you wanted to get something to eat before you settled in."

"Yeah, I do. I appreciate it, but I really need a favor." I expected him to look at me crazy, but he appeared to be cool.

"If it's something that I can do, I'll be happy to help."

"If you can't do it, I'll understand, but I really need to get my hair cut."

"That shouldn't be a problem. As a matter of fact, if you know a good barber, I need to get mine cut too," he laughed. Finding a good barber wasn't a problem. My cousin, Derrick, was the best to ever do it when it came to cutting hair.

After confirming our arrival with him, I directed Mr. Gibson to the barber shop that I owned. When we pulled up, I had to do a double take when I saw Keanna's car parked in front of the building. As bad as I needed my hair cut, I felt like saying fuck it and telling Mr. Gibson to pull off. I couldn't act a fool in front of my probation officer. That was a one-way ticket back to jail if I did.

This scandalous ass bitch better not say anything to me or I wasn't going to be responsible for what I did to her ass. I didn't care if she was my cousin. I appreciated her for calling me when she saw Alexus at the club with ole boy, but I still didn't want to fuck with her no more.

Derrick told me that he only had three customers, but he would take us as soon as we got there. The sooner he was done, the better it would be for me.

We walked through the door and I had to pause for a minute. No, this nigga, Malik, was not sitting up in the very same barber shop that I called my own. He had his head down, but I would recognize his punk ass from anywhere. When he looked up, we made eye contact and I saw the fear all over his face. He couldn't even look me in the eye without turning away. Damn, I wished Mr. Gibson wasn't in here with me.

"What's up cuz?" I asked, speaking to Derrick. I introduced him to my P.O., whom he instructed to sit down in his chair. Mr. Gibson sat in the barber's chair, while I sat down right next to Malik. He was trying to act like he was on his phone, but I could tell that he was nervous. He was in luck today. I had no choice but to give him a pass.

"How are y'all doing today?" my cousin, Derrick, asked us. Usually, he would be cutting up and acting a fool, but he knew how to play the part whenever he had to. Mr. Gibson spoke back as Derrick adjusted the black cape around his neck. Malik stood to his feet and pulled his keys from his pocket.

"I'm going make a run right quick Derrick. I'll be back in a minute," he said as he headed for the door.

That nigga was a hoe for real. I wasn't trying to do his scary ass nothing, but I guess he wasn't taking any chances.

Derrick nodded his head and continued cutting Mr. Gibson's hair. Malik bolted out the front door like somebody was after him and slammed it shut. I got up and looked out of the window to see which way he was heading.

"What the fuck!" I said out loud once I saw him get into Keanna's car and drive away. I wondered why her car was out front, but she was nowhere around. I'd be damned. Keanna was as trifling as they came. Now, I knew why she wasn't worried about Troy being locked up. She was too busy fucking Malik.

Chapter 13

I was so happy to be spending time with my best friend again. Jada and I were just leaving the nail salon after getting a pedicure and were now headed to my mama's house. We were supposed to go out to eat, but my mama wanted me to watch my sister's kids until she got home from work. She was supposed to be watching them but, whenever a man called, she dropped everything. Jada didn't want to come with me at first, but she changed her mind after I begged for over an hour. We decided to order pizza so I could feed my nieces and nephew too since I knew they probably didn't eat. I hated babysitting. My sister, Ayanna, started out working overnight; now, she claimed she was working double shifts. None of it made sense to me because she was just as broke now as she was when she first lost her job.

"Mama!" I yelled when I walked through the front

door.

I smelled her perfume, so I knew that she was about to dash the scene. As much as I loved my mama, this was the part of her that I hated. She acted so thirsty sometimes. It's like she had to have a man. And my sister, Ayanna, was just like her. The only difference was that Ayanna knew who all three of her kids were for and my mama didn't have a clue as to who fathered us. She claimed we all had the same daddy, but I knew that was a lie because we all looked different.

Our so-called father was a man named Max that she dated off and on until he died about seven years ago. She and Max dated throughout high school and he was her puppet, just like the rest of her men. He probably went to his grave thinking that we were his kids, even though none of us resembled him in the least. I always assumed that I was mixed with something because of my complexion and the texture of my hair. Two of my brothers had gray eyes and the other one had brown. My sisters and I had light brown eyes, but the resemblance ended there.

We were complete opposites in every way. They were both tall and slender with no curves at all, and I was shorter and shapelier. There was no doubt about where my shape came from. My mama had the best shape a woman in her forties could ever have and she knew it. She was so proud of my shape because I was the only one of her girls who actually took after her.

Men worshipped her like she was some kind of trophy and she loved it. She often encouraged me to be the same way, but that would never happen. As much as she hated Dre, she still encouraged me to get all that I could get from him. I was determined to do the opposite. I didn't want to depend on a man for the rest of my life. That was the reason why I was in school. I wanted a career so that I could take care of myself. The only time my mama worked was when she was in between men and wanted to get some extra money.

"Alright, I'm out of here," my mama said when she entered the living room. She was wearing the hell out of a leopard-print halter dress. The six-inch red heels she strutted in only made the dress look that much better. Anita Bailey was the shit and nobody could tell her otherwise.

"Did they eat yet?" I asked, even though I already knew the answer.

"Nope. And if their mama gets here before I get back, tell her that she needs to stay here with her own damn kids. I'm not babysitting this weekend, so she better not go anywhere," my mama said with an attitude.

"Does she have to work?" I wanted to know.

"I don't know, but that's her problem. I never saw a job where you have to work seven days a week with no off days. Knowing her, she might be laid up with some nigga. You know it don't take much to get her stupid ass to drop her pants. I know she better not bring no more damn babies up in here." My mama was still fussing as she walked out the front door. I felt the same way and I was happy to know that I wasn't alone.

"Why is she always so hard on Ayanna?" Jada asked with a frown on her face.

"Nobody is hard on Ayanna. She's always lying about where she's going so somebody can watch her bad ass kids," I replied. Just at the mention of my sisters' kids, her daughter came running into the living room.

"You better stop running in your grandma's house and sit down," I told her as she ran around the sofa.

"Lex, we're hungry," my niece, Shira, whined, looking over at me.

"I know. I'm about to order a pizza in a minute." She got up and walked over to Jada and started playing in her hair while I pulled out my phone and looked up a few pizza places in the area.

109

"Jada!" my other niece, Layla, yelled while running into the living room and jumping into Jada's lap. This was crazy. As much as they saw Jada, they never behaved this way. But, then again, she hadn't been around lately, so maybe they were happy to see her too.

"Can we spend the night at your house Auntie Jada?" Layla, asked.

Auntie? I thought to myself. That was a first. My nieces and nephews didn't even call me auntie. And when did they start asking to spend the night at Jada's house? Jada smiled, but she never answered. I looked at her and I could tell that they were making her feel uncomfortable so I stepped in.

"Y'all go back upstairs with your brother until the pizza gets here," I told them while pointing towards the stairs. My nephew, Tyran, was always on his video games, so he never bothered anyone.

"But we want to talk to Jada," Shira whined.

"I don't care. Go upstairs before I slap you!" I yelled at both of them. They were pouting, but they got up and ran up the steps.

"You are so mean," Jada said, shaking her head at me.

"Since when did you become so kid friendly?"

"You know I always did have a soft spot for kids. I just don't want any of my own."

That was so true. Jada couldn't pass a child without saying something to them.

"Whatever heifer. Let's order this food," I said, waving her off.

A half hour later, we were enjoying three pizzas with hot wings and bread sticks from our local Pizza Hut. My nieces were still clinging to Jada and they were getting on my last nerve, but I let it slide.

"So, what's been going on with you and your mystery man?" I asked her. We still hadn't had a chance to talk since we left the restaurant a few weeks ago.

"It's not a mystery, but we'll talk later," she replied, knowing later would never come.

"You told me-" I started to respond, but the ringing of her phone stopped me. She jumped up from the table and ran into the living room before she answered. I was tempted to follow behind her, but I didn't. Jada never hid anything from me so I just knew that something wasn't right.

"I gotta go," Jada announced when she walked back into the room. She didn't even finish eating and she was rushing out the door.

"Damn, you can at least finish eating before you jump at his commands," I said with an attitude. She ignored me and grabbed her purse, heading straight for the door.

"I'll call you later!" she yelled before closing the door behind her. I wouldn't hold my breath waiting for a call that would probably never come. I stood up and started clearing the table when I got a text message from my sister, Ayanna, saying that she would be working overnight.

"Fuck!" I yelled in frustration. Now, I had to be stuck inside watching her damn kids while she was out doing whatever because she damn sure wasn't working. I hated to do it, but I had to call Tyree and tell him that I couldn't come over tonight.

Chapter 14

I was so happy to finally be back at home. When I got out of the hospital, my mama insisted that I stay with her until I was fully recovered. I ended up staying in the hospital for three days after I lost my baby. The doctor had to do a dilation and curettage procedure, also called a D&C, to remove any abnormal tissues. They were also able to tell me that I would have had another little girl and that hurt like hell.

To my surprise, I wasn't as down as I thought I would be. Usually, I would be too depressed to eat or even get out of bed, but not this time. My kids kept me occupied most of the time so that helped a lot. I was even more shocked to hear from Dre. Erica told him about what happened and about the miscarriage, and he called to make sure that I was doing alright. He even expressed his sorrow for the loss of 'my baby', as he put it.

I was too embarrassed to tell anybody about what really happened to me, so I created my own version of the story. Instead of saying that I was beat up by my cousin-in-law, I told everybody that I was jumped by one of Dre's old flings and her sister. I didn't think before I said it and I'd been regretting it ever since. Now, my family hated Dre even more than they did before. According to them, it was his fault that I lost my baby. They blamed Dre for everything bad that happened in my life, but I didn't see it that way. I knew I'd made some bad choices in my life and I was paying for them now. Keanna was a different story and I would deal with her in my own way. I had a little bit of dirt on her and now was the perfect time to bring it to light.

"Mama, when can we go see our daddy?" my daughter, Denim, asked me.

Dre had been moved to a rehabilitation center not too far from here, but we still hadn't visited him yet. He wanted his brother to bring the kids to see him, but I refused to let them go. They wouldn't be going with anyone else but me, and I was going to make sure of that. He had to complete fourteen days of probation before he could have visitors and that was finished three days ago, so I knew that he was pissed about not seeing them.

"I don't know. We might go sometime this week," I replied. Well, I was hoping that we would go sometime this week. Erica told me that he had to wait another two weeks before he could get a pass to leave the facility. Hopefully, he wouldn't wait that long to see his kids.

"Auntie Erica is here!" Lil Dre yelled from the living room. Erica came to see me every day that I was in the hospital, but we hadn't seen each other since I'd been at my mama's house. I opened the door just as she was coming up the walkway.

"Hey boo. How are you feeling?" she asked as she gave me a tight hug.

"I'm good girl. Much better than I thought I'd be," I replied, hugging her back.

"That's good. My mama went saw Dre's stupid ass today. He's still asking us to bring the kids up there."

"Tell him that these are our kids, so he can call me if he wants to see them. I'll be happy to bring them for a visit." I never wanted to be the type of woman who used her kids to get a man's attention, but Dre left me no choice. While I appreciated him calling to check on me after I lost our baby, that wasn't good enough. He still refused to acknowledge the fact that he was the father. He needed to know that avoiding me was not going to make me go away.

"We told him what you said, but he is not trying to hear it. I told him that I was coming over here, so he's supposed to be calling to talk to them."

I assumed that was the reason for her visit, but I didn't say anything.

"It's not even that serious. So, he'd rather not talk to his kids before he calls my phone?"

"I guess so." Erica shrugged. That was just like Dre's selfish ass. He wanted everything to go his way, but I wasn't having it this time. Erica sat down next to me on the sofa, just as her phone vibrated in her hand.

"That's him calling now," she said.

"Put him on speaker phone," I whispered before she answered the phone.

"Hello." As soon as she answered, she put the call on speaker phone so that I could listen.

"What's up? Did you make it over there yet?" Dre asked her.

115

"Yeah, I just got here. Do you want to talk to the kids?" Erica put her finger over her lips, telling me to be quiet. I wasn't going to say anything because I wanted to hear what he had to say. Denim was the first one to the phone. Her lil ass was too grown and tried to walk away with the phone. I pulled her back and made her talk right in front of me.

"Hey daddy! I wanna come see you!" she yelled into the phone.

I wanted to see what Dre's response to that was going to be.

"I want to see you too, baby. I'm trying to get somebody to bring y'all up here," he replied.

Denim looked at me like she was waiting for me to say something, but I never did.

"My mama said that nobody but her is bringing us up there. Can she bring us up there today?" Denim asked. I had to remind myself to stop talking around her because she repeated everything that she heard.

"Y'all can't come today. The visitation hours are over."

I grabbed my daughter by her shoulders and whispered in her ear. I didn't want Dre to hear me coaching her on what to say. Once I finished telling her what to say, she nodded her head and proceeded to tell him everything that I said word for word.

"What time is visitation tomorrow? My mama can bring us to see you tomorrow." She looked at me for approval once she finished talking. I gave her the thumbs up, letting her know that she did it right. Dre didn't say anything and I thought he might have hung up.

"Hello," Denim said into the receiver.

"Yeah, I'm here baby."

"Please, daddy," Denim whined. "We wanna come see you." This time, I didn't have to coach her. She was doing all the begging on her own.

"Yeah, y'all can come see me tomorrow," he finally said after a long pause.

Excited was not even the word to describe how I felt. I knew that he couldn't go too much longer without seeing them and I was right. He spoke to the rest of the kids for a while, but he never asked to speak to me. After Drew talked to him, Erica got back on the phone at Dre's request. She was talking to him but looking directly at me, so I figured I was the topic of their conversation. Erica was quiet, making it obvious that he was doing all the talking.

"Alright, I'll talk to you later," she said after what seemed like forever.

"What did he say?" I asked her.

"He's pissed." I figured he would be, but I didn't give a damn.

"Pissed for what?" I asked like I didn't already know.

"He said that he don't know why you're trying to come see him so bad."

"I remember a time when he used to beg me to come see him when he was locked up. Now, he wants to act like it's a problem."

I couldn't even front; my feelings were hurt that Dre felt that way. No matter what we were going through or what we had already been through, I was still his wife.

"Well, he told me to give you the address and stuff so you can bring them up there tomorrow," Erica said. I got up and got a paper and pen for her. I was excited and scared all at the same time. I could never tell how a meeting with my so-called husband would go. I just had to pray for the best and prepare for the worst when it came to Dre.

I woke up extra early the next morning. I wanted to make sure that the kids and I were on point for when we visited Dre. I rolled my girls' and my hair the night before, so all I had to do was apply my make-up and get dressed. I always got the kids ready last to make sure they didn't get dirty before we left. When we pulled up to the facility, my kids were going crazy. They were so excited to finally be able to see their daddy. I sat behind the wheel of my car, trying to get my emotions in check. I saw Dre a few months back, but that was different. We were separated by a glass and had to use a phone to talk to each other. This time, we would be face to face and the thought of that made me nervous.

"Mama, let's go," Lil Dre said.

"Wait a minute boy. Y'all are too impatient."

I pulled out my compact mirror and made sure I looked as flawless as I did when I first left home. Once I was satisfied with my appearance, I opened my car door and got out. I helped my kids get out of the car and we all walked towards the entrance. The place didn't look like much from the outside, but the inside was simply beautiful. It almost had a tropical feel to it with all the palm trees that were in the lobby.

"Good morning. Can I help you?" the friendly receptionist asked me.

"Yes, I'm here to see my husband, D'Andre Mack," I replied. If I wasn't looking at her closely, I would have missed the slight frown that appeared on her face. It was quickly replaced with a fake smile that I could have done without.

"Ok. You guys can have a seat in the visitation room and he'll be right out," she said, pointing to a door to my left.

I grabbed Drew's hand and made my way to the room, with my other kids following close behind. The room was huge with a big tv mounted on the wall. There was a table with blocks and puzzles that quickly got the kids' attention. They sat down and started playing while I fidgeted nervously in my seat. We waited for about twenty minutes and I was just about to go ask the receptionist what was taking so long when the door swung open.

"Daddy!" Denim screamed when Dre walked into the room. The rest of the kids jumped up and ran over to him as well. I looked up at him and my breath was caught in my throat. He looked so damn good. I guess I was looking for the rough face and dingy orange jumper that I saw when I visited him a few months ago. That was not the case this time. His face was clean shaven and his hair was cut to perfection. His Polo outfit looked like it was fresh off the hanger. He picked Drew up and made his way over to a row of chairs on the other side of the room and sat down. I started to go off, but I held my tongue. He didn't acknowledge my presence at all, and I was offended.

"Well, hello to you too, Dre," I said after I made my way over to where he was sitting.

"What's up? I was coming speak to you," he said, looking up at me. I sat down in the chair next to him, but he got up before I had a chance to say anything. I was embarrassed, but I didn't show it. I wasn't about to chase him all around the room like a child, so I stayed where I was. The tv was on, so I pretended to be watching whatever was playing. The tears that were attempting to fall were blinked away rapidly because I refused to cry. For the next hour, I pretended not to notice my husband playing with our kids and completely ignoring me.

"What's wrong mama?" my daughter, Dream, came over and asked me.

"Nothing. I'm ok," I lied with a fake smile.

"You look sad," she observed while sitting on my lap.

No matter how hard I tried, I could never hide my feelings from my babies. They always saw right through me. I put my arm around her waist and welcomed my temporary company. I heard the door open and looked up to see the receptionist coming into the rec room with a few magazines in her had. She looked over at Dre and they shared a quick smile. When she turned to walk away, his eyes stayed glued to her ass the entire time. It didn't take a genius to know that either something was going on or it wouldn't be long before it did. Typical Dre. Nothing that he did surprised me anymore. As long as I never saw her around him, we wouldn't have any problems.

"So, how have you been?" Dre asked, sitting down next to me. I didn't know why, but the butterflies in my stomach were doing the most. My daughter, Dream, got up and went to play with her sister while we talked.

"I'm better, considering the circumstances," I replied lowly. I figured trapping Dre with another baby didn't work, so pity was my next best chance.

"Yeah, I've been meaning to ask you, what really happened when you lost your baby?" Dre asked me while looking into my eyes.

"I already told you what happened," I replied, looking away from his piercing stare. "And stop saying my baby. That was our baby." He looked at me like he knew that I was lying.

"I know what you told me, but that shit just doesn't sound right. You remember every single chick that I ever cheated on you with but, somehow, you don't remember this one." His tone was accusing and I didn't like the way that he was looking at me.

"First of all, I don't remember every chick you cheated with because it was too many to keep up. And why do I have to lie about something so stupid?"

"That's the point that I'm trying to make. But, if that's what you say happened, then cool. I can only go by what you say."

I was happy that he was leaving it alone because I was tired of explaining myself to him and everybody else.

"So, what's the deal? Why did you want to come up here so bad?" he asked, catching me off-guard.

I rehearsed my lines in my head over and over again, but I was at a loss for words once I was in his presence.

"We need to talk about us, Dre. Our family is falling apart and we need to find a way to fix it."

There, I said it and it felt good coming out. He looked away quietly, like he didn't know what to say. That couldn't have been the problem because he never had a problem saying what was on his mind. He sighed and turned to face me.

"Cherika, look, I thought a lot about us when I was locked up. I asked myself if getting a divorce was the right thing to do. I also asked myself if I could be faithful to you if we stayed together," he said, pausing.

I was feeling hopeful at first, but the next words he spoke broke me into a million pieces.

"I can't do it though. The damage is already done to this marriage and nothing can make it right. You deserve somebody that's gon' love you and be faithful to you. I'm not that man."

I couldn't stop the tears from flowing this time. This time wasn't like all the other times that he told me it was over. This time, I knew that he was serious. We weren't fussing or fighting. We were sitting down having a conversation like two adults. That was something that we'd never done before. He reached over and wiped my tears, but that only cleared a path for fresh ones to escape.

"Is it because of Drew?" I had to know why he was destroying the one thing that meant so much to me.

"Not at all. I love Drew like I love the rest of my kids. We haven't been happy with each other for a long time and you know that. I can't understand why you're still trying to hold on to something that's not there." He held my hand but that did little to comfort me.

"You never really tried to make it work Dre. The first thing that comes out of your mouth is divorce."

"What other options do we have?" he asked, sounding aggravated. "I'm trying to handle this the right way, but you're making the shit too hard."

He let my hand go and grabbed some tissues that were on the table, handing them to me.

"I'm not trying to make things hard. I just need you to understand how I feel."

"I already know how you feel. The whole damn world knows how you feel," he replied with a frown. I was not easily discouraged and begging was nothing new when it came to my husband.

"Please, can we just talk to somebody? If that doesn't work, I swear I'll leave it alone. At least I can say that we tried. You don't have to answer with him me now. Just tell me you'll think about it." I pleaded with him like I often had to. He still looked hesitant, but I wasn't taking no for an answer.

"I'll think about it Cherika, but I'm not making you any promises," he finally said after a long pause. I could tell that he only said what I wanted to hear, but that was still music to my ears. I smiled a genuine smile for the first time in a long time because I was truly happy. All hope was not lost. I would have my family back by any means necessary.

Chapter 15

"Why the fuck would you tell me to let your cousin cut my hair! Are you trying to get me killed?" Malik yelled.

"What the hell are you talking about?" I asked. I was lost, but something had him pissed.

"Don't try to play stupid. I'm talking about your cousin, Dre, coming in there looking at me all crazy and shit."

"Dre!" I yelled in surprise.

"Yeah, Dre," Malik said, mocking my tone. "That nigga walked in the shop like he owned it or something." Malik took a seat on my sofa and shook his leg nervously.

This was news to me too. Nobody told me that Dre was home. I hadn't talked to Eric since last week but, even then, he didn't mention it to me.

"Actually, he does own it." I laughed but he obviously didn't find humor in my reply.

"You think that shit is funny? It's because of him that I lost my job while you're sitting here laughing," he said, pointing his finger in my face.

I stopped laughing when I saw that he was really mad.

"I'm sorry." I lowered my head in shame. I knew that Dre was a sensitive subject for Malik. A few months back, Dre had my cousin, Quan, and some of his friends jump on Malik in a bar. As a result, Malik had to have his jaw wired shut. He'd just started a job three months before the incident, but they decided to terminate him after learning that he would be out for a few weeks.

Soon after that, his car was repossessed and he started to fall behind on his bills. He had an eviction notice on his apartment door yesterday and he'd been in a foul mood ever since. I tried to help him, but there was only so much that I could do. I let him use my car, but I couldn't offer him a place to stay. I was pushing it by even having him in the house at all. Troy would kill us both if he ever found out.

"Let's go somewhere. We can catch a movie or go out to eat, my treat." I wanted to do something to make him feel better since he always seemed to be in a bad place all the time.

"Naw, I don't want to go anywhere. I don't need us to run into any of those nosey muthafuckers that you know," he said, waving me off like it was nothing. I was so tired of him acting like he was embarrassed to be seen with me and I had to let him know it.

"I'm so sick of this same bullshit with you! I'm good enough to give you money and let you drive my car. I'm even good enough to suck and fuck you every time you ask, but it's a problem whenever I want us to spend time together outside of the house!" I yelled, standing to my feet.

Deep down, I knew that he was really worried about us running into Alexus and I was hurt. I was taking a huge risk by being seen with him too, but that never stopped me.

"You're so busy worrying about your ex bitch seeing us. That girl is not even worried about your stupid ass." I was pushing it, but I didn't care.

"See, this is the shit that I be talking about. You knew what it was from day one. I didn't come after you, you came after me," Malik said, pissing me off even more.

But he was right about that. I did pursue him. The night Dre went to jail was the same night that I ran into Malik at the club. After I dropped Eric off to pick up Dre's car, I decided to go back to the club and have a few drinks. Malik was still there, so it was the perfect time for me to make my move. I'd always thought that he was handsome, but Alexus had already sunk her claws into him before I ever got the chance to.

He didn't seem interested when I first approached him, but I wasn't taking no for an answer. After I convinced him to come outside with me, I took him around the back of the club and showed off my mind blowing oral skills. He ended up coming home with me that night and the rest was history.

It was cool at first, but things started to change soon after. I started out thinking that dating Malik would be a way to piss Alexus off, but that would never happen because he was too scared of being seen in public with me.

After a while, I ended up catching feelings for him and it was getting harder and harder to walk away. I thought I'd finally found a man who had his shit together, but I was dead wrong. Malik ended up being a scrub just like Troy. He was just a younger version with a degree. I didn't know how I always ended up with these broke ass, busted ass niggas. Something had to be wrong with me.

"I'm trying to see how I'm gon' pay my bills and you're worried about going out to eat," Malik said, interrupting my daydream. He was stretched out on the sofa like this was his house.

"I told you I'll see what I can do to help," I replied after a long pause.

"You can't do shit for me on that little bit that you make at that nursing home."

He had the nerve to frown in disgust when he said it. He always had something negative to say about my job, but that same job was the only reason why his broke ass still had a cellphone and lights.

"You're barely paying your own bills, so how can you help me?" Malik asked.

"I got my ways," I said, smiling at him. I wasn't proud of some of the things I did but, when Troy stopped helping me pay bills, I really didn't have a choice. I'd been working overtime for months just to make ends meet and that still didn't help.

"Whatever." Malik waved me off but I wasn't one to be dismissed. I walked over to the sofa and attempted to lie on top of him, but he wasn't having it. He grabbed my arms and held them down until he was sitting upright.

"Stop! I'm not in the mood for all that hugging and shit." He released my arms but I wasn't giving up. I leaned over and tried to kiss him, but he put his hand up and turned his head.

"Man, stop! I told you that I'm not with all that kissing and shit!" He yelled in frustration. This time, I was the one who wasn't trying to hear it. Malik claimed he didn't like to kiss, but I specifically remember his tongue staying down Alexus' throat when they were together, so I knew that was a lie.

"Make love to me again," I whispered in his ear. He looked at me like I was crazy and started laughing.

"Oh, so that's what you call it?" He was laughing hysterically but I didn't get the joke.

"What do you mean by that?" I was starting to feel played and his laughter only made it worse.

"Nothing. If you don't know, I'm not trying to enlighten you," he replied sarcastically.

I reached over and grabbed his belt buckle. Once I had it loose, I unbuckled his pants and pulled them halfway down. I reached my hands into his underwear and pulled out his semi-hard love stick. He looked at me and smiled as I stroked him up and down slowly. I was happy that I was wearing a dress. It would be easier for both of us that way. His eyes rolled to the sky as I slightly increased the speed of my hand and stroked him faster. Three minutes later, I stopped stroking and stood up directly in front of him. I bent over and wiggled out of my underwear and walked up to him with my dress lifted. I was about to straddle him and give him the ride of his life, but he stopped me before I had the chance.

"What?" I asked, looking at him in confusion. Malik was never very affectionate with me, but he never turned down sex either. I was about to curse his ass out, but I saw that he had other plans for me. He grabbed me by the back of my neck and forced me down to my knees. Before I had a chance to protest, he rammed his dick in my mouth, gagging me in the process. I tried to pry his hands from my neck, but his grip was too strong. Malik was moaning, but I felt like I was choking to death. I started moving my head from side to side until he finally let go.

"What the fuck is wrong with you?" Malik asked with an attitude.

"You're choking me to death; that's what's wrong," I replied with an attitude of my own.

127

"My bad," was all that he said before lowering my head for me to continue sucking him off.

As bad as I wanted to tell him no, something in me wasn't ready to be alone. So, like the fool I was, I sucked his dick just the way I knew he liked it. I had a feeling that this would be just like it was most of the other times. Malik would get some fire ass head and be too tired to do anything else. It was enough that I played the fool for one man but being a fool for love twice was more than I could handle.

Chapter 16

Retail therapy was just what I needed. So, when the twins called me to go shopping with them, I didn't mind at all. Tyree had been working a lot lately, so I was on my own more than I wanted to be. He and his dad had a lot of newly purchased properties that they were trying to get renovated, as well as some new clients that were in the market to purchase property. The long days and short nights were killing me, but I understood that his business came first. Even though doubt tried to creep in at times, I had to put my insecurities to rest and trust the man I loved. Every man was not like Dre and I had to keep that in mind.

I pulled up to the twins' house and blew my horn to let them know that I was outside. They were always driving me around, so I figured I could return the favor for once. They both came running out of the house and hopped in the car at the same time.

"Let's roll sissy. I got my ticket for my Jordan's, but I have to be there by noon or they're going to sell them," Trina said, holding up her ticket. She was the queen of Jordan's. Every pair that came out was added to her collection. I loved tennis too, but I would trade them any day for some cute heels.

"Girl, whatever," I said, waving her off. "It's not like you don't already have every pair that came out."

"It doesn't matter heifer. I need these for the block party Saturday."

"You're coming to the block party, right?" Tina asked me.

"I'm thinking about it," I replied. The twins and Tyree's uncle was a retired DJ who owned a record shop in Uptown New Orleans. I'd only met him once, but he invited me to his annual block party that he threw in front of his record shop to benefit needy kids in the area. Tyree basically told me that I was going, but I was still undecided.

"What's there to think about? It's for a good cause," Trina said.

We made small talk as we drove to the mall and prepared to shop until we dropped. My thoughts wandered back to all the drama that took place the last few times I was here and I almost wanted to change my mind and go back home. I would die if I ran into Cherika while I was here with Tyree's sisters. Her husband and I were through, but she still seemed to have a problem with me. She couldn't pass me by without saying something slick out of her mouth. She'd obviously won. After all, she was the one having another one of his babies as she so happily reminded me.

"Hello," Trina said, snapping her fingers in my face. I was so caught up in my thoughts; I didn't hear anything she'd said.

"My bad girl What did you say?" I asked, giving her my undivided attention.

"I was asking you which store y'all wanted to hit up first," she replied.

"It really doesn't matter. I'm not looking for anything in particular."

Of course, our first stop was to Foot Locker to get Trina's Jordan's. I was happy that we got that out of the way because we were sick of hearing her mouth. Tina and I went to Wilson's Leather and took advantage of their seventy percent off sale. I ended up getting three leather bomber jackets with the boots to match. This trip was turning out to be much better than I had anticipated. Most of all, it was drama free and that was something that I could get used to.

"I'm done, but I could damn sure use something to eat," Tina announced. We'd been shopping for almost four hours and I was done too.

"I'm starving," Trina said, agreeing with her sister.

"Do y'all want to eat here or somewhere else?" I asked both of them.

"We can eat here. It's not too crowded in the food court," Tina said as we made our way over to that area.

After a few minutes, we were all sitting at the booth, enjoying the Chinese food that we ordered.

"I just noticed that I haven't talked to Tyree since this morning," I said aloud to no one in particular. I reached into my purse and grabbed my phone to give him a call. I was trying to be understanding about his work load, but it only took a minute to pick up the phone to say hello.

"What's up Lex?" I heard someone say. I was almost scared to look up to see who it was. I knew it was too good to be true. Every time I came to the mall, I was met with some kind of drama. I finally lifted my head and smiled when I saw Trent standing in front of me.

"Hey Trent," I said as I stood up to give him a hug. Trent was my nephew, Tyran's, father. Even though he and Ayanna didn't work out, we were still cool. In the beginning, he was very active in my nephew's life, but he was always in and out of jail so much, and Ayanna got tired of the foolishness. Trent was my sister's first heartbreak and she never seemed to be the same after that.

"What's going on with your sister?" he asked.

"Nothing much. She's just been working like crazy," I replied.

"I've been calling her like damn near every day to get my son, but I see she's on that bullshit," he said angrily. I was under the impression that Trent was still locked up, so I didn't know anything about that.

"I didn't even know that you were home," I said, shocked by his comment.

"Man, I've been home for over a year. My mama and my sister have been trying to call her so we can see my son. She keeps putting us off with all these lame ass excuses. I don't want to have to go to that strip club and drag her stupid ass off the stage, but I will if I have to. She already know that I'm the wrong one for her to play with."

I know this nigga did not just say what the hell I thought he said.

"Wait, what do you mean the strip club?" I asked in surprise. He looked confused for a minute before he answered me.

"Honestly, I'm not trying to get into y'all family business, I'm just trying to see my son," Trent said with his hands raised. I decided not to push him for answers because I was gon' do some investigating on my own.

132

"Look Trent, I really don't know what's going on with you and my sister, but I can definitely make arrangements for you to see your son. Me and my mama always have them while she's at work."

"I would really appreciate if you could do that for me, Lex," he said, smiling.

Trent and I exchanged numbers, with me promising to let him visit my nephew the next time I had to babysit. Once me and my girls were done eating, we made our way to my car and stuffed our bags inside. The sun was setting and I had yet to hear from Tyree. I tried calling him twice, but I only got his voicemail. I was pissed and I could only wonder what his excuse was going to be for being MIA all day.

I was so aggravated. After I dropped the twins off home, I just wanted to take a nice long shower and climb into my bed. I wouldn't even mind all the noise that I knew my nieces and nephew were going to make. Any distraction was a good one as far as I was concerned.

"Are you coming in for a little while?" Trina asked me when we were around the corner from their house.

"No, I'm going home and relax," I said, feeling down. I wasn't in the mood to do much of anything right now. When I turned the corner, I had to do a double take when I saw Tyree's car parked in his parents' driveway. I saw a silver Honda Accord backed up behind his car, but I had no idea who the car belonged to. My heart dropped and I almost lost control of my car when I saw Tyree standing next to the Honda, talking to Mikayla. They were so deep in their conversation that they never even saw us pull up.

"What is he doing talking to that crazy bitch?" Trina asked as she and her sister jumped out of my car and started grabbing their bags.

"Don't trip Lex, he don't want her thirsty ass," Tina said as she retrieved some of her bags from the back seat.

133

"I'm so done with his dog ass," I said, looking straight ahead. I felt the tears building up and I knew, if I looked his way, they would fall whether I wanted them to or not.

For the first time since we met, I looked at Tyree in a different light. He tried so hard to convince me that he was so much better than Dre but, right now, he was doing a poor job of it. I guess me being happy was too good to be true. Once he looked over and saw his sisters getting out of my car, he started making his way over to where we were.

"Lex, let me talk to you for a minute," he said while rushing over to my car. I saw his movements from the corner of my eye, but I still didn't turn to face him. The twins got the last of their bags, just as Tyree got to the driver's side of my car.

"Baby, it's not even what you think. Her mama is trying to buy a bigger building for her restaurant," he said, almost in a panic.

I wasn't trying to hear nothing that he had to say. If it was that simple, he could have just told me that in the beginning. Then, to make matters worse, that bitch Mikayla had a smirk on her face when I looked in her direction. That really pissed me off.

"Fuck you, Tyree! I'm done," I said as I put my car in drive.

"Don't do this Alexus. Just get out of the car and let's talk," he pleaded. "I swear, I'm telling the truth; you can ask her."

"No, I'm good. Go finish talking to your future because I'm officially your past." I pulled off slowly and drove away.

"Alexus, wait! Alexus!" Tyree yelled to my departing car.

I was so hurt, but that was becoming the story of my life. That bitch named karma was at it again. I spent years with somebody else's husband, so it was only right for the same thing to happen to me. Even though I knew that was true, it still didn't take away the pain that I was feeling.

I tried not to cry, but I couldn't help it. The tears were coming at a rapid pace and I couldn't stop them. I pulled my car over because I could barely see since the tears were almost blinding me. I grabbed my phone and called the first person that came to mind. After ringing five times, Jada's phone went to voicemail. I tried three more times and got the same results, so I decide to leave her a message.

"Jada, it's me. I know that you're probably busy, but I really need you right now. Please call me back," I cried into the receiver.

Immediately after I left the message, my phone started ringing and I just knew that my best friend was calling me back. I frowned when I saw that it was Tyree instead. I sat on the side of road through five more of his calls before I finally felt good enough to drive away.

When Tyree saw that I wasn't answering, he started with the test messages. I read each one, but I wasn't about to respond. In just a matter of minutes, all the hurt that I felt before turned into anger. I was angry with Tyree for doing me wrong. I was angry at myself for even falling for him in the first place. But, most of all, I was angry with Jada. She still hadn't called me back and I was furious. So furious that, instead of going home, I decided to pay my best friend a visit. After tonight, best friend was a title that would no longer belong to her.

I pulled up to Jada's house about fifteen minutes later. There were no lights on, but I knew that she was home because her car was in the driveway. It was a little after seven, so she couldn't have gone to bed this early. Whatever the case was, I was ready to get down to the bottom of it. As much as I loved my friend, I hated how weak she had become behind a man.

I got out of my car and made my way up the stairs to Jada's front door. I was about to ring her doorbell, but I decided to use the key that I kept on my key ring. Our friendship was over as far as I was concerned, so I didn't care if she got mad. I pulled the key from my key ring because I would be leaving it here since I had no use for it anymore. I didn't want to hear any more excuses. I couldn't remember a time that I wasn't here for Jada and she was always here for me. Lately, all of that changed and I was tired of trying to figure out why.

I opened the front door and was met by the sweet scent of candles as soon as I walked in. That was no surprise. Jada loved to light incense and candles throughout her house. There was a lamp on in the dining room and a small light shining over her stove in the kitchen. The house was fairly quiet, with the exception of the soft music that was coming from upstairs. I guess Jada was entertaining, but I didn't give a damn. I was hurting in more ways than one and I was about to break up her little party.

As I got closer, I heard Floetry playing, followed by what I knew was Jada's voice. Here I was in pure misery and she was laughing it up without a care in the world. Some damn friend she was. I saw the flicker of candles coming from underneath the door as my hand rested on the doorknob. I took a deep breath in an attempt to calm my nerves. It was too late to turn back now, especially since I'd come this far. I turned the doorknob and walked in, not knowing what to expect.

"Jada?" I called out as I walked into the room. I saw two naked figures intertwined on top of the covers, but it wasn't until they separated that I figured out who it was.

"Oh, my God!" I yelled while covering my mouth with both of my hands. Suddenly, the room was so small that I couldn't breathe. All the walls were closing in on me as I backed out of the room in shock.

"Oh, God! Lex, wait!" Jada yelled, trying to cover her naked body.

Had I not seen it with my own eyes, I wouldn't have believed it. My sister, Ayanna, and my best friend, Jada, were lovers? I couldn't believe it, but there was no mistaking what I just saw. Ayanna jumped up and grabbed some clothes that were scattered on the floor.

"Couldn't you call first before just letting yourself in someone's house?" my sister snapped angrily. My voice was caught in my throat, so I couldn't tell her that I did try to call. Four or five times to be exact. I took the steps two at a time until I was back in the living room.

"Lex, wait please," Jada cried. She caught up with me just as I made it to the front door.

"Can you just listen to me please?" she said while grabbing me by my shoulders. I jerked my body sideways until she was no longer touching me. I reached into my front pocket and pulled out her house key and threw it at her.

"You were right! I don't understand and I do hate you," I said as I walked out of her house. The look on her face let me know that my words hurt her more than she could say. I really didn't mean it, but I was hurt and I wanted to hurt her in return.

I jumped into my car and sped away from Jada's house as fast as I could. For the second time that day, I was betrayed by someone who was supposed to love me. It was crazy, but I was more hurt by Jada than I was with Ayanna. Over the years, I'd learned to expect the unexpected with my sister, so nothing that she did surprised me anymore.

It was all starting to make sense to me now. That was why my nieces were asking her to spend the night at her house. They'd probably been there several times before. I guess I knew whose kids Jada was babysitting now. I often wondered where they went when they weren't with me or my mama, but the mystery had been solved.

Once again, my phone was ringing off the hook. Jada and Tyree were taking turns draining my battery, but they were both wasting their time. As bad as I wanted to go home, I decided against it. I didn't want or need my ex-boyfriend or my ex-best friend to show up apologizing. I needed a drink and I was on the hunt for one at the moment.

I drove around for thirty minutes before I finally ended up on South Claiborne Ave. at Jazz Daiquiri Lounge. The place wasn't in the best part of town, but they sold some of the best drinks that money could buy. I parked my car directly in front of the door and made my way inside. Jazz was famous for their fruit loop daiquiri, so I ordered myself one and made my way to an empty table.

A few men tried to flirt, but I ignored them all and kept walking. My phone was still going crazy with calls and text messages. Even though I didn't answer the calls, I read all the text messages, just to see what everybody had to say. Tyree and Jada were both begging me to call them, but that wasn't happening any time soon. Ayanna was the only one who didn't reach out and that was fine with me. My head was down and I was so engrossed in my phone that I didn't pay much attention when someone walked up to my table.

"You look like you could use some company," a male voice said standing before me.

"Aww shit," I mumbled as I looked up into the smiling face of none other than D'Andre Mack.

Chapter 17

Well, I'll be damned. My first weekend pass home and I was definitely in the right place at the right time. I'd just dropped my kids off at home after spending the day with them and decided to go get me a drink. I was just about to leave when I spotted Alexus walking through the door. I knew her so well that I could tell that she had been crying the minute I looked at her. I waited before I approached her, just to make sure she was by herself. Alexus never traveled alone, so I knew that something had to be wrong. For some reason, she had been on my mind a lot lately so this had to be fate.

"This can't be real. There is no way in hell that my day can be this fucked up," she said, burying her face in her hands.

"What's wrong baby girl?" I asked as I took a seat at her table. I hadn't been gone that long, but I missed the hell out of her for the short period of time that I was away from her. She was still the prettiest chick that I ever laid eyes on, and I couldn't stop myself from staring at her.

"Don't call me that Dre. And don't sit at my table. I see a bunch of empty tables in here, so you need to go pick one," she snapped. I shook my head and laughed at the attitude that she was trying to give me. Not much had changed. Alexus would forever have that flip ass mouth, no matter what.

"Damn. I'm just coming over here to make sure you're alright. I can tell you've been crying. You want to talk about it?"

"No, I don't, but thanks for asking."

"What, you and your new man having problems already?"

"Don't worry about me and my man. And for your information, we are fine."

I felt some kind of way about her admitting that she even had a man in the first place, but I played it cool. I decided to fuck with her since I knew for a fact that she was sitting up in my face lying to me. There was definitely trouble in paradise and I wasn't stopping until I found out just what was up.

"So, where is he? It's almost ten o'clock and you're sitting in a bar having drinks by yourself. Not to mention, your phone has been going off like crazy since I walked over here."

I had her right and she knew it. She snatched her phone off the table and threw it in her purse.

"Where's your side kick, Jada? Why is she not in here with you?" That was rare for them not to be together, especially if Alexus was having problems. Jada was always there for her.

"Fuck Jada," she spat, taking a huge gulp of her drink. Now, I knew that shit had to be real. She used to be with Jada damn near more than she was with me. That was one of the problems we had when we were together.

"What happened"?

"Nothing happened Dre. Just leave me alone."

"Alright, but at least let me buy you another drink," I said, standing to my feet. I walked over to the bar and ordered both of us a drink while Alexus stayed at the table drowning in her sorrows. Under the rules of the facility that I was in, I wasn't supposed to be drinking at all. But, just like my ex, I had a lot on my mind too.

I didn't know why, but I agreed to go to counseling with Cherika and I'd been regretting the decision ever since I made it. I really didn't understand why she even wanted to be with me so bad. Even I knew that I wasn't right for her. She would never have me all to herself and she knew it. The sad part was, she was alright with that.

"When did you get out?" Alexus asked me when I came back to the table.

"I'm not really out," I replied, handing her the drink I bought for her.

"What, you escaped or something?" She looked at me sideways like I had done something wrong.

"No." I laughed before I explained everything to her. "My P.O. got me in a program, so I didn't have to do all of explained to her.

"Oh, so when do you get out?"

"If things go right, I might only have about thirty days left, maybe less. The waiting list for the facility that I'm in is kind of long, so they might be letting a few of us out early."

She picked up her cup and gulped down some of her drink. I knew that something was bothering her but, at the rate she was going, she would be drunk in no time.

"You might want to slow down with that drinking, love. You know that drinking was never your thing." I looked at her, expecting a flip response that never came. To my surprise, she lowered her head and burst out crying. I jumped up from my chair and moved to the chair that was closest to where she was. I grabbed a handful of napkins from the table and handed them to her.

"What's wrong Lex?" I asked her as I pulled her chair closer to mine. I always did hate to see her cry, even if it was my fault sometimes.

"Everything is wrong," she cried, leaning her head on my shoulder. She smelled so good, but now wasn't the time to make my move.

"It can't be that bad." I rubbed her back in comfort. She sat up straight and gave me a cold stare.

"Yeah, well, you're not the one that just caught your sister and your best friend in the bed fucking either," she said sarcastically. This time, I was the one who was staring at her.

"Ayanna?" I asked, surprised.

"Yes, Ayanna." She frowned when she said her sister's name.

"Damn. I knew that Jada got down, but I never thought your sister was that type," I said, shaking my head.

"What the hell you mean you knew Jada got down? Got down with what?" She gave me a crazy look.

"Come on now Alexus. I know you're not that damn naïve. You have never seen your girl with a man before. How do you think she met Keanna?" I assumed she knew everything about her girl, but I was obviously wrong.

142

"Keanna mess with girls too?" she asked loudly.

"Damn, you really didn't know, huh?"

"Didn't know what? You're driving me crazy with all these riddles." I could tell that she getting angry so I told her what was up.

"Keanna and Jada used to mess around. I thought you knew. Why do you think they don't get along now? Keanna was feeling some kind of way when you and Jada got tight, so they went their separate ways."

"What! Wasn't Keanna with Troy though?" She seemed to be genuinely shocked.

"Yeah. That nigga knew what was up, but he didn't care. And now I know why he didn't care."

I guess he didn't care that his girl was fucking with other girls since he was too busy fucking with other men. I still didn't know how that got past me for so long.

"It's like I don't know who is who anymore. Nobody is who they say they are." Lex shook her head like she was really confused by it all.

"Everybody's not like that. I was always real with you, no matter what. You were the one that did me wrong," I said, looking her in the eyes.

"You can't be serious. You call fucking me and your wife at the same time being real?"

"I wasn't fucking y'all at the same time. I left Cherika to be with you and look where that got me. If I wouldn't have been chasing behind your lying ass, I probably wouldn't have went to jail in the first place!" I was getting heated just thinking about it.

"It's not my fault that you went to jail, so don't blame that shit on me!" she yelled back.

"Yeah, alright. You probably be fucking with that same nigga that you was in the club with the night I went to jail. Tell the truth for once in your life. You can at least give me that."

"Why does it matter who I'm with? We are not together."

"You don't have to keep saying that. I already know. I don't even want to be with your sneaky ass no more," I lied. I was hurt so I wanted to say anything that I thought would hurt her too.

"I don't want to be with you either," she said seriously.

"Cool, so now that that's out of the way, answer my question." I looked deep into her eyes awaiting an answer.

"What question?" she asked, as if she didn't already know.

"Is the dude that you're with now the same dude that my brother saw you in the club with a few months ago?" I asked loud enough for her to hear.

"Yes," she replied with her head down.

"Yeah, that's what I thought. So, where is he now? It must not be all that good if you're out her by yourself this time of night."

"That's not your business. He's not like you, so he doesn't have to go everywhere I go."

"That's bullshit and you know it. That nigga did something wrong. I know you, Alexus. If y'all were straight, you wouldn't even be in here right now." She knew that I was telling the truth, but she didn't respond.

"Don't get quiet now. You left me to be with that nigga and now it's not what you thought it was gon' be," I said, rubbing it in. I didn't know what the nigga did, but I was happy that he did it.

144

"I didn't leave you to be with nobody. I left you so you could be with your wife."

"Stop lying. You knew what the deal was with me and Cherika. Hell, you came with me when I had the divorce papers drawn up. If that wasn't what you wanted, you could have said something a long time ago." I was getting pissed off all over again.

"I did say something. I tried to leave you a million times, but you wouldn't let me. You made me sneak and lie and cheat. You wouldn't let me have a life if you weren't in it," she said with tears streaming down her face.

I thought about what she said. Maybe I did go about things the wrong way, but that still was no excuse for how she did me.

"Alright, I'll take the blame for some of that, but you fucked over me big time and you know it. I couldn't even get you to pick up the phone when I called and you knew I was locked up. Then, you went like a thief in the night and moved all of your stuff out of the house."

"That was the only way that I was able to get away from you, Dre. If you wouldn't have gone to jail, you wouldn't have let me leave."

"Fuck outta here with that. You talking like you were a prisoner or some shit."

"That's exactly how I felt."

We both sat there, staring at each other in silence. I didn't know how we ended up talking about us, but I was happy that we did. At least, now, I knew how she felt. As mad as I was, it still didn't change how I felt. She was still my heart and nothing would ever change that. Not even my wife.

"So, now what? That's just the end of me and you?" I asked her.

"Yes, Dre. I finally have some peace in my life and I want it to stay that way. Up until all of this happened today, I was drama free. And, besides, you just said that you didn't want me anymore anyway."

"So, you never had peace when we were together?" I asked, ignoring the last part of her statement.

"Not as long as your wife had breath in her body, I didn't."

"Well, you don't have to worry about that anymore. That's a wrap." I was trying to convince her to give me another chance, or at least think about it.

"You always say that but, the truth is, you want us both."

"No, I only want you."

"Yeah right. You want the best of both worlds. You want to play around with me in the day and go home and screw your wife at night."

"I wasn't even having sex with her when we were together, so that's a lie."

"Well, how did she get pregnant if you weren't having sex with her?" I was caught off guard with that one. I didn't think she even knew about my wife being pregnant. Knowing Cherika, she probably sent her the sonogram to make sure she found out.

"Who said it was mine?" I asked, looking at her.

"She made sure I knew it was yours, so don't even try to lie," she said, looking right back at me. There was no sense in me lying, so I didn't try.

"So, this makes baby number five huh?" she asked.

"Nah, she had a miscarriage." I was sorry about what happened to Cherika, but I was relieved that I wouldn't have to go through even more drama by having another baby with her.

"Sorry to hear that," Alexus said apologetically.

"So, where are you staying at now? I'm guessing it's with ole boy, huh?" I braced myself for the answer that I wasn't sure I wanted to hear.

"No, I live with my mama, but I'm not going there tonight. I don't want to run into Ayanna or nobody else."

"Well, I know you're not going by Jada, so where are you going to go?" She had a faraway look in her eyes and I hated to see her so sad.

"I'll probably go by my brother for a few days. I just need to get away."

"Well, you know you're more than welcome to come chill at the condo by me. At least while I'm home for the weekend," I suggested. I looked at her, expecting to see her frown up, but she never did. She actually looked like she was thinking about it, but her words said something different.

"Thanks for offering Dre, but I don't think that would be a good idea."

I was persistent, so I wasn't trying to hear that. She was vulnerable, but I would take her any way I could get her right about now. It was wrong, but that's how I felt.

"Well, let me put you up in a room then. What about the Ritz-Carlton on Canal St.?"

I knew that was her spot. Before I bought us the condo, we used to chill there all the time.

"I can't. I don't even have any more clothes with me." I knew it was all good when she said that. Any other time, she

147

would have flat out said no. I was excited like a kid at Christmas, but I didn't show it.

"Don't worry about that. I'll take you to get something tomorrow."

She didn't say anything, but I could tell that she was thinking about it. I didn't want to seem too pushy, so I didn't say anything else. I waited until she was ready to reply.

"Alright Dre, but don't think you're staying there with me. Just pay for the room and leave."

"That's cool," I said, throwing my hands up in surrender.

"Once I make sure you're straight, I'm leaving," I lied. There was no way in hell I was leaving that room once I paid for it. She stood up and grabbed her purse and her drink before heading for the door. I snatched up my drink and followed close behind her while quietly admiring the view. I didn't know who her man was, but I was definitely about to give him a run for his money.

Chapter 18

Things weren't perfect in my world, but they were certainly looking up. It took a lot of persuading on my part, but Dre had finally agreed to go to marriage counseling with me. I couldn't believe that he actually said yes. He was so unpredictable at times. I didn't want to give him a chance to change his mind, so I was sitting in my living room with my sisters, looking through the phone book for some counselors in our area. I wanted to do it before Dre got released from the facility he was in, but that was proving to be harder than I thought.

I figured that if everything went right, Dre might move back home once he was released next month. He still didn't tell me that he might be coming home soon, but Erica kept me on top of everything that was happening. He was currently enjoying his first weekend pass home, but I hadn't seen much of him. He spent all day Friday with the kids, but nobody knew where he was today. He promised to come back for them today, but he never answered his phone when I called. Erica said that he was probably running the streets with Eric, but my woman's intuition told me something different.

"That nigga still not answering his phone?" my sister, Charde, asked me.

"Nope. I know he see me calling him too," I said, heated.

"He's wrong for that shit. He know these children be looking forward to seeing him."

"Did you try calling from a different number?" my sister, Cherice, asked.

"No, he knows all of y'all numbers, so he's still not gon' answer," I replied.

"Knowing him, he's probably laid up with somebody," Cherice said, shaking her head. I hated to admit it, but she was probably right. Dre still had his condo so that was where he was staying while he was home. I swear, if I knew where it was, I would kick that door down and stomp whatever bitch he was in there laid up with.

"He might be laid up with that hoe Alexus," Charde chimed in.

"No. He ain't laid up with her. She found another sucker to take care of her. It's probably somebody he just met with his dog ass." I was getting mad just thinking about it.

"You're always saying that he's a dog, yet you're looking through the phone book trying to find a marriage counselor," Cherice said sarcastically.

"I know but, if this doesn't work, that's a wrap. I'm tired of trying." I said that more to myself than anyone else. I love Dre more than life itself, but I was wearing myself out chasing behind him.

"You should be tired. Especially since you're the only one who seems to be trying to make it work," Charde chimed in.

"Bitch, I suggest you keep your mouth shut. You're really not in a position to give me any advice on my husband," I said, pointing my finger in her direction. She looked away without responding and that was the best thing for her to do.

"Don't get mad with her. You're not mad with Dre's dog ass. He's just as much to blame as she is," Cherice said, taking up for our sister.

I found out a few months ago that my sister, Charde, gave my husband oral sex, but that wasn't the worst part. I assumed it happened only once. Imagine my surprise when I found out that it had been going on for months. I forgave her, but she could keep her opinions about my husband and my marriage to herself.

"I'm not mad at nobody. I just don't want to hear that shit right now." I had an attitude and I didn't try to hide it.

"Mama, is my daddy coming to get us today?" my daughter, Denim, asked when she entered the living room. She had been coming in and out of here every five minutes asking the same question.

"You are getting on my last damn nerve asking the same question. Get out of my face and go upstairs somewhere!" I yelled. I could tell that I hurt her feelings, but I really didn't care at the moment. Dre had me in a fucked up mood as usual.

"You shouldn't have hollered at her like that Cherika. It's not her fault you're mad with her daddy. You need to stop letting what he do control how you feel," Cherice said.

"Like I just said, I'm not mad with nobody. I'm just tired of her coming in here asking the same question."

"Girl, let's get out of here before I say something that I might regret," Cherice said to Charde. They both got up and headed for the door at the same time. I didn't care one way or the other. I wasn't in the mood for company anyway.

"Call me when you get your attitude together," Cherice said before slamming my front door.

I felt bad for the way I was acting, but I couldn't help it. The person that I wanted to get mad at was nowhere to be found, so I lashed out at those who were close around me.

I laid on my sofa, rubbing my now slightly flattened stomach while deep in thought. I wondered how things would have been between Dre and me if I'd had our baby. There was no doubt in my mind that things would have been different. Dre loved kids, so I knew that he would have come around eventually. Unfortunately, thanks to Keanna, I would never know.

My blood boiled every time I thought about the fight we had that caused me to lose my baby. Even after I told her that I was pregnant, she still kicked me while I was down. She was hurt and I knew all too well how she felt, but my unborn baby's health should have meant something to her. Hate was a strong word and an even stronger emotion, but I really hated her for what she did to me.

I felt the warm tears glide down my face at a rapid pace. I was so tired of crying, but that was all that I seemed to do lately. I got up from the sofa and grabbed some paper towels from my kitchen counter to wipe my face. A thought came to me and I was about to act on it before I changed my mind. I sat on my living room floor, flipping through the phone book until I saw what I was looking for. I dialed the number and waited for someone to pick up the phone.

"Uptown Health Care," a woman said after the phone rang three times.

"Hi, I'm calling to speak to the Director of Nursing," I said in my most professional voice. I was told to hold while my call was being connected. I decided that today would be the last day that I shed any tears. It was time for me to get back to the way I used to be. I hope everybody was prepared because I was done being nice.

Chapter 19

I didn't know how I made it back to work in one piece, but I did. I'd just gotten off at six that morning and was back at two that afternoon to work a double. I was here damn near more than I was at home. The overtime money was nice, but my side hustle money was even better. I needed every penny I could get. Helping Malik out was wearing me down. It was like taking care of two households, instead of one.

Malik went job hunting every day, but he still hadn't found anything yet. He had a few promising interviews and I hoped like hell somebody hired him soon. I didn't know how much longer could I do this, especially since Troy would probably be home any day now. Even though he was given six months, he most likely wouldn't have to do that much time. The jail was already overcrowded, so they were releasing nonviolent offenders left and right. He would kill us both if he knew what was going on.

As hard as I tried not to, I ended up catching feelings for Malik. I didn't plan on giving him up when Troy came home, so I would have to find a way around it. Sneaking around wasn't going to be a problem for Malik, since he wanted to keep our relationship hidden anyway.

I walked into the break room and went straight to my locker. There was a note taped to the front, so I pulled it off before I opened it. Once I secured my purse in my locker, I sat down and read the note that was attached.

"Aww man," I sighed as I read what the letter said. My supervisor, Tanya, whom I hated by the way, called a meeting right before I was scheduled to clock in. I was pissed because I would have to stay at work longer to make up for the time I'd miss. She was always calling these boring ass meetings, just to remind everyone that she was in charge. I hated to pull into the parking lot and see her car there. Some bullshit was always sure to follow.

"Hey girl," my co-worker, Donna, said when she entered the break room.

"Hey," I spoke back. "I guess you have to stay longer for the meeting huh?"

"What meeting?" she asked, stopping in her tracks. I showed her the letter that was taped to my locker and watched as she read over the contents.

"I didn't get a letter, so I guess whatever she has to say doesn't apply to me. I've been here for sixteen hours and I'm tired. I'm not staying a minute longer for none of her boring ass meetings. Don't even tell anybody that you told me. I'll see you tomorrow," she said as she exited the break room.

I knew that feeling all too well, so I didn't blame her for running out of here. I got up from the table and started making my way to the empty board room where all of our meetings were usually held. When I got there, Tanya was already there, along with two other women whom I'd never seen before.

"Have a seat Ms. Mack," Tanya said.

Before I had a chance to sit down, Kelly, one of the nurses that I worked with, came into the room and was instructed to sit down too. Immediately, I knew that something was wrong. Kelly was an LPN, so she was never in the same meetings as the CNA's. We made eye contact and I could tell that she was wondering what was going on, just like I was. We didn't have to wonder for long because Tanya started talking as soon as we were both seated.

"I know that you're both wondering why I called you in here, so I'll get right to the point. Mrs. Smith and Mrs. Landry are here from the Louisiana Board of Nursing. Some discrepancies have been brought to our attention concerning some of the patients' medications," she said all in one breath. Kelly lowered her head, but I looked straight ahead without showing any kind of emotion. Tanya grabbed a stack of papers and continued talking.

"I have paperwork that was signed by the both of you, stating that medicine was administered to patients that they never received. Some of the paperwork is dated back to last year. We also show that medicine was still being signed out for some patients who had passed or were no longer in the facility at the time.".

I was numb. There was no getting out of this. We were busted and they had the paperwork to prove it. Working like a dog for sixteen hours a day still wasn't enough to make ends meet so, when Kelly approached me with a great idea, I took her up on her offer.

Some of these patients slept all day every day, but they were being prescribed sleeping pills. Some of them were on their death beds but were being fed high dosages of pain pills. So, instead of giving them what we felt like they didn't need,

Kelly and I would sign the medicine out and keep it for ourselves to sell. According to her, there was no way that we could get caught. She was obviously wrong. I couldn't understand how they found out what was going on. I didn't know who Kelly talked to, but I'd only told a handful of people and those were the ones who I sold the pills to. They would never tell if it meant not getting them anymore.

Tanya was still talking, but I was oblivious as to what she was saying. I looked over to my left and saw Kelly bawling like a baby, so whatever she was saying couldn't have been good. It was of no use to me to sit here any longer and I made it known.

"So, now what?" I asked defiantly. Mrs. Smith looked at me and shook her head in disgust before she replied.

"What happens now, Ms. Mack, is on top of you being terminated, your CNA License is being revoked indefinitely. The only reason why you're not being prosecuted is because your supervisor declined to press charges."

That came as a surprise to me. I always thought that Tanya hated me, but I guess I was wrong. Not only was I being fired, but I wouldn't be able to work as a CNA anywhere in Louisiana without a license.

"Anything else?" I asked with sarcasm lacing my voice. Tanya looked at me like I was crazy before she responded.

"No, that's all. The security guard will escort you to your locker to get your things. You'll also need to leave your I.D. card and keys with him before you leave."

I stood up and almost ran to the door that led me out of the room. I was greeted by our security guard as soon as the door opened. I handed him my badge and keys as he followed me to my locker. Once I was done, he escorted me out of the building and locked the door. When I got to my car, there was an envelope under the windshield wipers. I removed it and threw it in my purse that was now resting in the passenger's seat. Even though I tried to put on a brave face in the meeting, I was a wreck inside. This job was my only source of income and now it was gone. Troy was going to kill me. He knew what I was doing to get extra money for us, but he was still going to be pissed. Malik would definitely have to find a job soon because I couldn't do a damn thing for him without a job.

Before I realized it, I felt the warmth of the tears as they glided down my face. I usually wasn't one to cry, but so much was going wrong in my life lately and I really felt alone. With all the wrong that I'd done to others, I guess karma was bound to catch up to me sooner or later. A knock on my window scared me back to reality. I looked up and saw another one of my co-workers, Lisa, standing there looking at me pitifully.

"What's wrong chick?" she asked in a concerned voice. Lisa was cool, but I didn't consider her a friend. We'd worked together for about a year and I still didn't know much about her.

"Besides just getting fired, I'm fine," I said, looking up at her.

"Damn, I'm sorry to hear that, but I wouldn't be crying over that shit. That little money they paying ain't nothing." She waved me off like it was no big deal.

"Maybe not to you, but I have bills."

"And I don't?" she asked, pointing at herself. "I have four kids, boo. Trust me when I say that I have way more bills than you do. But today is my last day too. I just gave my notice," she said with a huge smile on her face.

I wondered what kind of job she had found. I knew that she had kids, but I never knew she had four. Then, she'd just bought a new car a few months ago, and she was standing here smiling.

"So, where do you work at now?" I asked curiously. "I might need a hook up."

"At She She's," she answered proudly.

"The strip club!"

"Yes, the strip club. Don't sleep on it boo. I make more there in three nights than I made here in two weeks. My brother is the bouncer over there, so it's safe. I can get you on if you want me to. All you need is some sexy lingerie."

"As bad as I need a job, I'll still have to pass on that one."

"Well, you know the number if you change your mind. They're looking for some new faces, so you need to think about it," she said as she walked off.

Lisa wasn't the prettiest girl I'd ever seen, but she had a shape that any woman would die for, including me. She had enough ass to last her a lifetime, while mine could barely fill out a pair of jeans. She could make a lot of money with the body she had, but I wasn't so sure about me. I had a cute face but, besides my ample breasts, I wasn't much in the figure department.

I sat there deep in thought, but it didn't take long for me to figure out that stripping would probably be my only option for now. I called Lisa and told her that I was on board. She told me what time to meet her at the club and what I needed to bring with me. Needless to say, I didn't have anything that I needed, so a trip to the mall was in order. I only had about three hundred dollars before I was completely broke, so I hoped Lisa was right about me being able to make money.

I pulled up to the Macy's entrance at Lakeside Mall and killed my engine. I took a deep breath, desperately trying to compose myself before I went inside the mall. There was no turning back once I spent my last three hundred dollars, so I had to be sure that this was what I really wanted to do. It was now or never. I got out of the car and headed for the double doors. I saw a car that looked familiar to me, but I had to get up close to be sure. Just like I thought, it was indeed who I assumed it was.

"What's up Dre?" I asked as I walked up on the driver's side of the car. He looked up and frowned as soon as he saw who it was speaking to him.

"Girl, if you don't get your ratchet ass away from my car," he said with disgust written all over his face. I was taken aback for a minute by his attitude. He was all nice and sweet a few months ago when I called to tell him about Alexus being in the club with another man. I guess if it wasn't benefitting him, he didn't want to be bothered.

"Damn, I was just hollering at you. You don't have to do all that," I said in my own defense. I wanted to ask him when he got out, but he made that impossible for me to do. He rolled up his windows to let me know that he was done talking. I kept walking and entered the mall, preparing to get what I needed. I headed straight for the lingerie department and was surprised, yet again.

"Hey girl. What are you doing in here?" I asked as I walked up on Alexus. She was also in the lingerie department, paying for her purchases. She looked me up and down like she didn't know who I was. I was about to say something else, but she stopped me with what she had to say.

"Let's get a few things straight before we go any further. I don't need you to tell Tyree anything about me and Dre. If I want him to know something, I'll tell him myself. I know you got a little crush on him and all, but he's way out of your league so let it go. You already know that you don't want it with me, so mind your fucking business. And while you're at it, get your life bitch," she snapped.

"And you're in the wrong mall. They don't have a Rainbow in here," she laughed.

She grabbed her bags and left me standing there looking like a damn fool. I should have known that Tyree was going to tell her what I said. She had him trained the exact same way that she had Dre. And thinking of Dre, a thought had just crossed my mind. It couldn't be a coincidence that they were both in the same place at the same time unless they were together.

I turned around and headed for the same door that I walked through a few minutes ago. I didn't go all the way back outside because I didn't want to be seen by anyone. I made it to the door just in time to see Dre's car backing out of the parking lot with Alexus in the passenger's seat. *Bingo!* I said, smiling to myself. She was just in here checking me about one man but was riding around with the other. I kept saying that Alexus was a hoe, but nobody seemed to believe me.

I turned around and headed back to the lingerie department with a huge grin on my face. It was going to be very interesting to see how this all played out. Dre was not the type to play the role of a side piece and I didn't think Tyree was either.

Thirty minutes later, I was walking up to the register with over one hundred fifty dollars' worth of lingerie. I made sure that I bought items that I already had shoes to match. I reached into my purse for my wallet and pulled out the envelope that was left on my car instead. I didn't know what it was, but my mind took me back to when I'd left a copy of the paternity test on Dre's car.

Curiosity got the best of me, so I got out of the line and sat in a chair that was next to the register. I opened the envelope and pulled out the letter that was inside. Someone had printed a copy of the different locations, days, and hours that the unemployment office was open. At the bottom of the letter, the words 'CHECKMATE BITCH' was written in bold red letters with the letter 'I' being dotted with a heart.

It didn't take long for me to figure out who that someone was and I was surprised that I didn't think of it before. Cherika was the only person that I knew who dotted her I's with a heart. She was also one of the few people who knew what I was doing at work. I sold sleeping pills to her and her sisters on several occasions.

I put the letter back in my purse and resumed my position at the register. I smiled as I thought about how much heart Cherika actually had. Of all the people that ran across my mind, she was not one of them. I should have known that she wasn't just going to go away so easily, but I definitely underestimated her this time. It was all good because I had a million more tricks up my sleeve just for her. It was crazy how she played the game and won with everyone else, but she kept losing when it came to her husband. She had one thing right though; 'Checkmate Bitch' because the next move was definitely on me.

Chapter 20

I was going crazy trying to get in touch with Alexus. She wasn't answering any of my calls or text messages. I knew that her seeing me with Kayla didn't look right, but it was all business and nothing more. She didn't even give me a chance to explain before she was ready to call it quits. I was mad at the fact of her even assuming that I cheated. I was tired of telling her that I was nothing like her ex, but she couldn't see it.

Jada had been blowing her phone up too, but she wouldn't answer for her either. I knew that she was alright because she kept in contact with my sisters. I damn near stalked her mama's house trying to see if she would show up there, but she never did. I was begging my sisters to try and get her to come to my uncle's block party this weekend so we could at least talk about it. They told me that they asked her a million times, but she was still undecided. I'd been sleeping by my mama's house for the past few days, thinking that she might show up here but that never happened. I was posted up in the dining room recliner watching tv like I'd been doing for the past few days.

"You need to bring your ass to your own house," my dad fussed when he walked into the room. "I told you to tell that girl what was going on before this happened, but you didn't listen to me."

He was right, but I wasn't in the mood for the 'I told you so' talk.

He told me to tell Lex that I was working with Kayla before I even started. I didn't do it because I knew that she wasn't going to be happy about it. I was pissed with him too. If he would have helped Kayla and her mama instead of asking me, then none of this would have happened in the first place.

"It's all good. I'm done working with Kayla and her mama. If they need help, they better call you," I said with an attitude. I braced myself because I knew that my pops was about to go off. He didn't play when it came down to the business.

"Check this out. If running a business and having a relationship is too much for you, just let me know. I can do this shit by my damn self. If your hard-headed ass would have been honest from the beginning, none of this would have even happened," he replied, going off on me.

I just sat there and let him say what he had to say without responding. I was stressed to the max, so I didn't have any more fight left in me. When my dad was finished schooling me, as he called it, he left me alone with my thoughts once again. I grabbed my phone and did something that I'd been doing for the past few days; I called Alexus.

"What do you want Tyree?" Alexus said when she picked up the phone. She sounded like I was the last person in the world that she wanted to talk to, but I didn't care. I was just happy that she picked up.

"Alexus, we really need to talk," I replied.

"No, we're good. We don't have anything to talk about."

"Man, stop being so childish and at least let me explain. It's not even what you think it is."

"So, let me get this straight; I don't talk to you for hours, you never answered when I did try to call, but when I do see you, you're outside your mama's house with your ex-girlfriend, and I'm being childish? And you're the same nigga that's always preaching about honesty?" she asked sarcastically.

"If you just let me explain, I'll tell you everything." I was already getting frustrated with this back and forth shit.

"Your first reaction to all your problems is to run away and that only makes things worse."

She held the phone for a while but didn't respond. I moved the phone from my ear to make sure she didn't hang up. Her picture was still on my screen, so I knew she was still there.

"Hello," I said, breaking the silence.

"Yeah, I'm here," she replied softly.

"When can I see you? We really need to talk about some things."

"I don't know Tyree. I'm at my brother's house and I probably won't be home until the weekend."

That was perfect. I could try to close the deal with Kayla and her mama and be done with them before the weekend came.

167

"Are you coming to the block party Saturday?"

"I don't know; I told your sisters that I would try."

"I really need you to come. It's cool if you don't want to stay, but we need to see what's up with us. Can you please do this one thing for me?"

I was stepping all the way out of my character with this begging shit. Usually, I would have no problem moving on, but this time was different. I really did love Alexus. In fact, I was in love with her. I wasn't willing to give up on us before we really had a chance.

"What time?" she asked, causing me to smile. All hope wasn't lost after all.

"Three o'clock," I replied.

"I'll be there."

That was music to my ears. It would be all good once we were face to face. It was hard trying to plead my case over the phone.

"Cool, so I'll see you this weekend," I said, happily.

"Ok."

"Lex, wait," I said before she hung up.

"What?"

"I love you." I held my breath, hoping that she wouldn't hurt my feelings.

"I love you too," she replied after a short pause.

I hung up the phone feeling like a new man. I was always telling Lex about the importance of honesty and it was definitely time for me to start practicing what I preached. We promised to always be honest with each other. She was living up to her end of the bargain; it was time for me to start living up to mine.

Chapter 21

I really hated myself right now. Here I was downing Tyree for not being honest with me, and I was straight up lying to him. I wasn't at my brother's house. In fact, I hadn't seen my brother in about 2 months, but I wasn't worried about him finding out the truth. My brother lived in Laplace, Louisiana and he didn't come to New Orleans unless he was coming to visit us and that wasn't very often. I was laid up in Dre's bed, yet again. A place I swore I'd never come back to. I wanted to blame me sleeping with him on the alcohol, but I was fully aware of what I was doing. One day was considered a mistake, but we were now on day number four.

When I saw him at the bar a few days ago, I ended up telling him about what happened with my sister and Jada. I left out the part about seeing Tyree with his ex. He didn't need anything to rub in my face later. He offered to pay for a hotel room for me and I agreed, but I somehow ended up coming back to the condo with him and I'd been here ever since. Dre was only out on a weekend pass at the time, so he hadn't been here with me the whole while. He'd only been allowed to leave on four hour passes on the weekdays, and he spent all four of those hours at the house with me, just like he was doing right now. He got pissed when I answered my phone for Tyree, so he left out of the room while we talked.

I was already starting to feel like I was making the same mistake all over again. Not much had changed since Dre and I broke up. Cherika was still calling him every five minutes and he still lied to her every time she called. He kept asking me to go places with him, but I would die before we got caught in public together. It was bad enough when I ran into Keanna in Macy's a few days ago. I was so happy that I was alone. Seeing me with Dre would have only given her more ammunition against me. I made sure to tell her messy ass about minding my business. This was her first and last warning from me. The next time something like that happened, I was whooping her ass, no questions asked.

I still had feelings for Dre, but I was in love with Tyree and that's who I wanted to be with. I didn't lie to Dre about anything. I didn't go into details about what happened with us, but he knew that Tyree was still my man. After our brief talk earlier, I was ready for us to put the past behind us and move on. He was right when he said I ran away from all of my problems.

I wasn't very confrontational when it came to my feelings, but I needed to get better. Even the situation with Jada and my sister was handled wrong. I didn't know if I could ever accept them being together, but I wasn't willing to lose my best friend over it. I finally answered the phone when she called me earlier. We were meeting up today so that we could have a much-needed talk. I really missed my friend. I was prepared to hear her out, as well as forgive her. After all, I was far from perfect.

"The next time you want to talk to your lil boy toy, you need to be the one to leave out of the room," Dre said while sitting down on the bed.

"I don't have a boy toy, I have a man," I replied.

"You keep saying that, but you've been in my bed for the past four days. Where was your so-called man at then?"

This was one of the reasons why I was having regrets about coming here in the first place. Dre could be an asshole sometimes. He wasn't accustomed to being number two. Cherika laid out the red carpet and threw rose petals at his feet, so he expected that kind of treatment from every woman. He already knew that would never happen with me.

"You are so right, but we're good now. I'm going back home today." I smirked, just to piss him off.

After I met up with Jada, I was going home to talk to my sister. So many things weren't adding up with her. I still couldn't get over Trent saying that she worked in a strip club.

"Fuck that nigga. He can have his fun with you for right now, but you're not going nowhere and you know that," Dre replied arrogantly.

"Watch me," I said, getting out of the bed. I grabbed my duffle bag that I bought from Macy's a few days ago and started packing up my clothes. True to his word, Dre made sure that I had everything I needed while I was there.

"I'm not talking about you going home. I'm talking about you leaving me alone altogether. No matter who you mess with, you gon' always come back to me. You can't stay away and neither can I."

I didn't reply because in some ways, he was right. Dre and I were familiar to each other, but it would never work out with us.

"Dre, even if I wanted to be with you, your wife would never let that happen. I told you that I'm done with all that

173

fighting and shit. You already have a complete family and I haven't even started one yet. I'm good with who I'm with." He looked like he was offended, but I was only being honest. I went in the bathroom and started grabbing all of my feminine items. When I turned around, Dre was standing right behind me. I jumped when I saw him and he smiled in return.

"So, you're saying that it's officially over between us?" he asked while closing the bathroom door.

"Yes and it really shouldn't have started back up. You're still married and I'm with somebody else. This is a disaster waiting to happen. Especially if your crazy ass wife finds out," I said, backing away from him.

The more I backed away from him, the more he came at me. After a while, I was backed into the wall with nowhere else to go. My mouth was saying one thing, but I was about to do the exact opposite.

"Why are you so worried about Cherika all of a sudden? It's not like you're scared of her as many times as you beat her ass. You're really worried about your dude finding out. That's what all the hesitation is about."

I didn't respond. Honestly, I was terrified of what would happen if Tyree found out that I cheated on him. Even though I saw him with Kayla, I had no proof that anything had happened between them. I only used that as an excuse to justify my wrong doings with Dre. When Tyree and I first got together, he asked me a million times if I was sure that I was over Dre. And a million times, I lied and told him that I was.

"I just feel bad for cheating on him," I said sadly.

I wish I could have taken what I said back, but it was too late. The damage was already done. Dre took a step back and looked at me with confused eyes.

"Did you feel bad for cheating on me with that nigga?" he asked angrily.

"That was different; you had a wife," I said in my defense.

"That' bullshit! I treated you better than any woman I was ever with, including my wife. Me being married was always your excuse whenever you got caught doing something wrong."

"You are really crazy. You get mad every time I bring up the fact that you're married. It's not like I'm lying. Let me get out of here; I'm not trying to get into an argument with you about facts."

I tried to move around him, but he blocked me from doing so. He pushed me back against the wall and grabbed both my hands, pinning them above my head with one of his. With his free hand, he reached under my night shirt and started to remove my underwear. I tried to close my legs, but he forced them open with his knee.

"Dre, stop. You gon' make me late," I whispered. It was crazy how my mind was saying one thing, but my body was saying the total opposite. Of course, he ignored my weak pleas and managed to get my underwear off with little effort. When he leaned down to kiss me, the little fight that I did put up was all gone. He didn't need to hold my arms down anymore because I wasn't going anywhere. When we broke our kiss, we stared at each other for what felt like forever.

He was too damn sexy and resisting him was almost impossible. My eyes drifted to the large, red colored letters spelling out my name that adorned his neck. Dre kneeled and wrapped one of my legs around his neck. I closed my eyes and grabbed the back of his neck as he dove in head first. All the guilt I felt earlier was long gone, but I knew that it would return once I came down off this high that Dre had me on.

Two hours later, I was seated at a booth in Chili's, the restaurant where Jada and I were meeting up. I was a few minutes early, but I used that time to think about a few things. I felt so bad for cheating on Tyree with Dre. I didn't know what kind of spell Dre had on me, but I needed to break it before it was too late. I looked down at the key that Dre had given me right before I left his house earlier. When he went to jail, I moved all of my things out of the condo and gave the key to his brother. I hated to admit it, but I'd be lying to myself if I said I would never use it again.

"Hey," a familiar voice said from behind. I turned around and saw Jada standing there, looking a bit nervous.

"Hey," I replied, feeling just as nervous as she looked. She sat at the booth across from me and picked up the menu. I picked mine up too and started looking over the appetizers.

"Are you ladies ready to order?" the waitress asked when she approached our table.

"I am," I said.

"Me too," Jada chimed in. We placed our food and drink orders and she disappeared just as quickly as she came.

"So, how have you been?" Jada asked me once we were alone.

"I've been better," I admitted.

"I know that I'm the cause of a lot of what's going on with you, and I'm so sorry. I wanted to tell you so many times, but I was scared. I didn't want our friendship to end over this."

"That's a really poor excuse Jada. I've never judged you. As much wrong as I've done, I didn't have room to. I've always been there for you, no matter what because that's what real friends do." She nodded her head but didn't reply.

"I just want to know how it all started. I mean, I never even knew that you were interested in women."

Now I knew why she was always so secretive about her relationships.

"Yes, I'm very interested in women and I'm sorry if that bothers you."

"Jada, you're my best friend. I don't want you to ever apologize for who or what you are. I love you regardless. It doesn't matter to me if you date a man or a woman. I just don't understand how you ended up with my sister."

"It's a long story. I ran into her one night at the store. She told me that she came to pick you up from school that day, but you left with Dre instead of her. Apparently, y'all had some words and she was upset. I invited her over so that we could talk about it. I didn't think she got down with women, but she was actually the one who made the first move. I swear, I didn't mean for things to go this far."

"Like I said before, you're my best friend and I love you, regardless of what you do. I just don't know how I feel about you being in a relationship with my sister."

"We're not in a relationship. In fact, we're not even messing around anymore. I made that clear to her after you left the other day. It's just not worth it to me." I was so relieved to hear that.

"I'm sorry for saying that I hate you. You know I didn't mean that."

"I know and I forgive you. Now that everything is out in the open, I just want us to go back to the way we use to be."

She looked so down and I hated it. Jada was usually so happy and playful. I would do anything to put that smile back on her face.

"I agree and all is forgiven here too," I replied happily. That seemed to do the trick. The smile that I loved so much had reappeared and I was happy to see it return.

"So, are we keeping your love life a secret or what?" I only asked because I didn't want to say something to the wrong person. I needed to make sure that telling anybody was alright with her.

"Not at all. I'm not ashamed of who I am and I hope that you're not ashamed either," she replied with confidence in her voice.

"Hell no! I'll never be ashamed of you. They can take it or leave it. As for me, I'll take it," I said, smiling.

She smiled back at me and I felt like a huge weight had been lifted. I had my best friend back and I couldn't be happier. The easiest part was over; my sister was an entirely different story.

I didn't know why, but I was kind of nervous when I pulled up to our house and saw Ayanna's car in the driveway. Ayanna and I weren't as close as most sisters were. She was always so negative and critical when it came to me. She always seemed to be jealous and I didn't know why. I helped her out whenever I could, whether it was financial or otherwise. I watched her kids whenever she needed me to, but nothing was ever good enough for her.

I got out of the car and slowly walked up the steps that led to our front door. I was dreading this confrontation, but it had to be done. I heard my nieces making noise as soon as I opened the front door. I saw Ayanna stretched out on the sofa when I entered the living room. I was about to sit down in the recliner so that we could talk. Before I had a chance to sit down or say anything, she went off on me.

"So, it's cool for you to fuck another woman's husband, but it's a problem when I do what I want to do, right?" she spat, stopping me in my tracks. I was shocked by her words, not to mention she said them in the presence of her children.

"Y'all go upstairs and play in Grandma's room," I told my nieces and nephew. They jumped up at the same time and headed for the stairs. Once I heard the door to my mom's room close, I went in on my sister.

"Bitch, don't get it twisted; I don't give a damn who you sleep with or what you do!" I yelled.

Chenell Parker

"Obviously, you do. I'm sure it was you who told Jada to end things between us."

"No, she's just like all of your babies' daddies; she don't have no more use for your nasty ass," I smirked. I was hitting below the belt, but so was she.

"Fuck you, Alexus!" she screamed, standing to her feet.

"Nah, I don't get down with girls. Hell, until a few days ago, I didn't think you did either. At least we don't have to worry about you getting pregnant again."

She walked towards me with fire in her eyes. I prayed that she didn't try to swing because I was prepared to lay her ass out. Sister or not, she could get it.

"And to think I came here to make peace with your jealous ass," I said, shaking my head. I didn't want to fuss or fight with her, but I intended to finish whatever she started.

"Nobody is jealous of you, hoe. You fuck any nigga that you think got a little change, married or not!"

"And it kills you to be working in that dingy ass strip club for all those hours and still don't have as much as your little sister, huh?" She looked at me in shock, probably wondering how I found out about her little secret.

"Yeah, I know all about your little night job," I said, making air quotes with my index fingers. "Mama was right when she said that you were stupid."

I walked past her and took the stairs two at a time, trying to get to my bedroom as quickly as possible. The tears were threating to fall, but I didn't want her to see them. I felt so bad about everything that I'd just said to my sister and regret was starting to set in. That was the thing about words; you couldn't take them back once they were said.

Chapter 22

It took me almost 3 weeks, but I was finally able to get Dre and I an appointment with a marriage counselor. I found her by doing a search of qualified doctors in our area, and we were meeting with her this afternoon. She only worked one Saturday out of every month and she was booked up for months to come. Lucky for me, she had a cancellation for this Saturday and was able to squeeze us in.

Dre seemed a little hesitant when I told him about the appointment, but he promised to be there. He had about ten more days in the facility before he would be released to come home for good and I couldn't be happier. I had a good feeling about us going to see Dr. Reynolds. Her track record was amazing. According to her website, in her ten years as a marriage counselor, she had a seventy-two percent success rate.

That meant that over half of the people that she helped ended up staying together. She was also a mother of four and had been married for thirty years. If anyone could help us get our marriage back on track, she was the one.

"Mama, we're here!" I yelled when I walked into my mother's house. She was keeping the kids until Dre and I came back. I was hoping that both of us could spend the day with the kids since Dre was home for the weekend. I guess that all depended on how well things went with our first session.

"Hey, my babies," my mama said, entering the living room. She hugged and kissed my kids before they ran upstairs to play. Since I had a few minutes to spare, I decided to sit down and talk to my mama for a while. We disagreed on just about everything, so it was rare for me to do that.

"Well, don't you look pretty today," my mother said, complimenting me.

I put a lot into getting ready for today, so I was happy that she noticed. I had my hair cut and colored yesterday; plus, I'd gotten a new outfit that complemented my figure very well. My manicure and pedicure were both freshly done this morning, so I was on point.

"Thanks Ma," I said, smiling.

"So, y'all are going to marriage counseling huh?" She didn't miss a beat. I knew that she was going to bring it up and I was prepared.

"Yes, we are. It'll do us some good to talk to somebody neutral. Dre thinks that we need a fresh start," I lied.

"Is that so?" she asked sarcastically. "So, if this doesn't work out, then what?"

"What do you mean, then what?" I hated when my mama did things like this. She never saw the good in anything when it came to my husband.

"Why do you always have to be so negative? Dre is trying, at least give him credit for that."

"There's a big difference in being negative and being honest."

"Well that's your opinion and you're entitled to that." I wasn't trying to be disrespectful but I had to speak my mind.

"I'm just tired of seeing you get hurt Cherika. Dre does not want to be married, but you can't seem to accept that."

"If he didn't want to be married anymore, he wouldn't have agreed to go to counseling. I didn't put a gun to his head."

"He probably agreed just to shut you up. I'm sure you had to ask more than once."

I'd heard enough. I was there for a good twenty minutes and I was ready to go. This was the reason why I didn't visit as much as she wanted me to.

"I have to go," I announced, getting up from the sofa. "I'll be back as soon as I'm done."

My mother followed me to the door, so I knew that she wasn't finished with her lecture. She grabbed my arm and forced me to face her.

"Why don't you and the kids come with me to church in the morning?"

"I don't know, Ma. They might be with Dre."

"Well, you can come by yourself," she said, not giving up.

"I don't know, Ma; I'll let you know." I hurried out the door before she could start up with another lecture. I wasn't in the mood for church unless it was to pray for my family to get back together.

I rushed to my car and pulled off, heading to one of the most important appointments of my life.

I got out of my car and made my way into the office building. I was thirty minutes early, but I didn't mind. I was a nervous wreck. I tried calling Dre three times, but he didn't answer once. I hoped and prayed that he showed up today. It was hard enough securing a Saturday appointment in the first place. I signed our names on the appointment form and took a seat in the waiting area. There were a million pamphlets scattered on the table in front of me that caught my attention. I picked up a few different ones and started reading over some of the contents. The advice that was given seemed so easy, but marriage was anything but. I thought I was doing everything that I was supposed to do, but I was obviously wrong.

I looked at the time on my cellphone and saw that we only had about five minutes before our appointment time. I was on the verge of tears because Dre still hadn't shown up nor answered any of my numerous calls. I was tempted to tell the receptionist to reschedule us, but I couldn't be sure if he would show up for another appointment either. I was ready to run out of the office and get in my car when the back double-doors opened and a pretty, petite lady stepped out into the waiting area.

"Hi, I'm Dr. Reynolds. You must be Mrs. Mack," she said, extending her hand for me to shake. I took her out reached hand and shook it. "Is Mr. Mack joining us today?"

I was so embarrassed. I couldn't believe Dre played me like this. Before I could answer, the door chimed, alerting us of a visitor. I wanted to jump for joy when I saw Dre walking through the door. He looked so damn good; I had to stop myself from staring at his tall muscular frame. It didn't matter that he was late; I was just happy that he showed up.

"Sorry I'm late," he said, looking at me and Dr. Reynolds

"You're actually right on time. Let's go to my office," she said, motioning towards the double doors. I got up and followed behind her with Dre hot on my heels. We walked down a long hall until we came to a door with her name on it.

"Come in and have a seat. I'll grab us some water and we can get started," Dr. Reynolds said before exiting the room.

Her office was small, but it was nicely decorated with two small sofas and a huge leather chair. There were also 2 smaller leather chairs against the wall. I sat on one of the sofas, while Dre occupied one of the chairs.

"Thank you for coming." I was smiling hard as hell at my husband.

"I told you that I would." He shrugged his shoulders like it was no big deal. We sat there in awkward silence until the doctor came back into the room. She handed us both a bottle of water and took a seat in her oversized leather chair.

"Okay Mr. and Mrs. Mack, let's get started. Who wants to go first?" she asked while looking at both of us. Dre just sat there, looking like he'd rather be anywhere else but here.

"I guess I will," I spoke up once I saw that he wasn't going to say anything.

"Well, Dre and I have been together for almost ten years, but we've been married for almost eight. There's been a lot of infidelity throughout our relationship and we're just trying to find a way to get past it and make it work," I said, looking at Dr. Reynolds.

Dre had his arms folded across his chest, looking at me like everything that I said was a lie. The doctor scribbled down some things on her legal pad before she spoke again.

"So, which party is responsible for the infidelity in your marriage?" She asked us both but her gaze fell on him.

"Both of us, but mostly my husband."

"Why do you say that it's mostly your husband?"

I felt like a spotlight was shining on me the way they were both staring at me, but I kept talking anyway.

"Because he can't seem to be faithful," was my simple reply.

"What do you have to say about that Mr. Mack?" she asked, peering at Dre over the rim of her glasses.

"Nothing," he replied nonchalantly. Dr. Reynolds removed her glasses and looked directly at Dre before she spoke.

"So, you don't have anything to say about your wife saying that you can be faithful?" I looked over at him as well, awaiting his answer.

"No. If she knows that I can't be faithful, why does she still want to be married to me?"

"Because I love you and I want us to be a family again. We had that until Alexus came along!" I didn't mean to snap but I couldn't help it. He was not about to make me feel bad for wanting my family to stay together.

"Who is Alexus?" Dr. Reynolds asked.

"The woman that he cheated on me with for over two years."

"I see." She wrote a few more notes on her legal pad.

186

"Is that true?" she asked, turning to Dre.

"Yep," he simply replied. He was pissing me off with these one-word answers.

"Mr. Mack, do you even want to be here?"

Dr. Reynolds seemed to be annoyed with his lack of participation. He obviously didn't want to be there and I guess she sensed it too.

"I mean, she asked me to come, so I came. Honestly, I really don't see the point of us coming to counseling. I don't think nothing is going to change."

"You don't know what the future holds. I'm trying my best to change, but you have to change some things too. I haven't had a drink in over a month and I've enrolled in night school to get my GED." I was trying and I needed him to meet me halfway.

"That's what I've been trying to get you to do for years. Why did it take me leaving for you to want to better yourself?" Dre yelled. I couldn't answer his question because I didn't know how. Dre was constantly on me about going back to school or doing something with myself. I never took it seriously because I never thought I would be without him to take care of me.

"So, it sounds like you're taking some steps in the right direction Mrs. Mack, but I have to wonder why," Dr. Reynolds said. "You need to make sure that you're doing this for you and not just to win your husband back."

I wanted to slap that bitch in her mouth for saying that. It really shouldn't matter why I was doing it as long as it was getting done.

"Let me just tell you what I see so far. This is only our first time meeting, but I can clearly see that you don't want to be here," she said while pointing at Dre. "That's the first step to making this work. Both parties have to be in agreement and I don't see that here. It looks like you both want something different."

I wanted to scream after she said that. I couldn't believe this bitch was calling herself a professional marriage counselor.

"I don't think that's it. Like I said before, Dre needs to learn how to be faithful and we'll be alright. Since Alexus is finally out of the picture, I think we can make it," I spoke up.

I was trying hard to convince Dr. Reynolds, as well as my husband.

"So, how do you know that there won't be another Alexus? Or how do you know that she's really out of the picture?" she asked.

I really hadn't thought about that. As far as I was concerned, Alexus was the only thing holding my husband back from being fully committed to me and our marriage. It never occurred to me that he could find someone else. And I didn't even want to think about her still being in the picture.

"I know for a fact that she's out of the picture. She cheated on him and left him for another man when he went to jail." My reply was petty but I didn't care. I wasn't only answering the doctor's question; I was also reminding Dre of what Alexus did to him.

"So, is she really out of the picture Mr. Mack?" Dr. Reynolds asked Dre.

I looked at him, awaiting his answer, but it never came. He dropped his head without replying. I knew right then and there what the answer was. He was back with that bitch. After everything that she did to him, he was back with her, but he couldn't forgive me for messing up one time.

Then, just like the last time, the ever-permanent reminder of her that was etched on his neck became visible. I hated that tattoo on his neck just as much as I hated her.

"Are you fucking serious right now Dre! What is it going to take for you to leave this bitch alone? Are you trying to drive me crazy?" I yelled.

"Calm down Mrs. Mack. I know that it's not the outcome that you wanted, but at least you know what you have to do now," Dr. Reynolds said, pissing me off even more. I hoped she wasn't talking about a divorce because that was not happening at all.

"Are we done?" Dre rudely asked.

"I guess we are, if none of you have anything else to say," Dr. Reynolds answered.

Dre stood up and started walking towards the door. I was so embarrassed and I was sick and tired of feeling this way.

"Thanks for seeing us," I said to Dr. Reynolds as I stood up and prepared to make my exit.

I really wanted to say thanks for nothing, but I held my tongue. I hurried down the long hall and through the double doors. I walked to my car, feeling defeated once again. Dre was only a few steps behind me, so I slowed my pace and allowed him to catch up. When he was close enough, I turned around to face him.

"Why did you even agree to come here with me?" I asked as tears rolled down my cheeks.

"I don't even know the answer to that question myself. I'm just confused about a lot of shit right now."

"This is not fair Dre and you know it. She did the exact same thing that I did, but you took her back just like that," I said, snapping my fingers. "I messed up one time and you're trying to make me suffer for it and it's not fair." I started crying harder and it was hard for me to stop.

He was looking at me with pity in his eyes, but he didn't respond. I almost expected him to walk away and leave me standing there, but he didn't. He surprised me when he pulled me into his arms and gave me a tight hug. I hugged him back just as tight, like my life depended on it and it actually did. Sometimes, I felt like I didn't want to live if I had to live without him. I knew that it was selfish of me to feel that way, but I couldn't help it. I'd never loved anyone the way I loved my husband. Dre let me go and wiped my face with the back of his hand. I looked up in his handsome face and had to stop myself from kissing him. I was too afraid of him rejecting me.

"The kids asked if both of us could take them somewhere today," I lied. "Maybe we can take them to the zoo or something."

I looked at his face to see his reaction. I could tell that he was hesitant, so I pushed even more.

"Please Dre," I begged. "We never do anything with them together."

"I guess so," he finally replied after a short pause. "I'll call you later."

He walked away and headed to his car. I had a smile on my face a mile long. I guess things weren't so bad after all. For the second time in a few weeks, I got Dre to agree to something that I wanted to do. To me, that was a step in the right direction. This was Dre's last time being home on a weekend pass before he was released. If I had my way, he wouldn't be spending it alone.

Chapter 23

I felt like I was back at square one with Cherika. I didn't know what the hell made me agree to go to this counseling shit in the first place. Then, I made matters even worse by agreeing to spend time with her and my kids. My kids weren't the problem, but she most definitely was. She put another guilt trip on me and I took the bait.

I hated to see a woman cry, especially if I was the cause of it. I really didn't want to lead her on, but she was making the shit too hard. Part of the guilt I felt was because I knew that she was right about some of the things that she said. Alexus fucked me over big time, yet I still rolled out the welcome mat for her. With Cherika, I used her cheating as an excuse to leave her alone. All I needed was a reason and she gave me a damn good one.

I knew it was selfish of me, but part of the reason I

wanted to keep Cherika around was to have a backup plan just in case things with me and Lex didn't work out. That was the only reason why I didn't pursue the divorce, even though I still wanted one. It didn't help that she threw the pussy at me every time I saw her. After she got pregnant that last time, I was scared to touch her. She almost got me one night when I dropped my kids off home, but I was happy I didn't go there with her, especially since that was the same night that I ran into Alexus. I guess her and her dude must have been having some problems because she ended up spending the weekend with me at my condo. That was the time I was supposed to be having with my kids, but I gave it to her instead.

Even when I went back to the facility, she was still staying at the house. Every day I was given a few hours to leave, and I spent all that time with her too. It was almost as if we picked up right where we left off.

Things were cool at first, but that didn't last too long. She ended up making things right with her nigga, and I almost had to make an appointment just to see her. It was like she had me working around this nigga's schedule and my stupid ass was actually doing it.

And she gave the nigga mad respect. Whenever he called, she broke her neck to answer the phone, making sure I stayed quiet in the background. I really was not that nigga and I couldn't believe that I was allowing her to play me the way she was playing me. It was cool for now though. I had a few days left before I came home and things were about to change. One thing I knew for sure; I was not cut out to be no side nigga and I didn't plan on being one for long.

I still had Mya, the girl who worked the front desk at facility, but she wasn't anybody special. She wasn't wifey or girlfriend material. Mya was cute, but sex was all that she was good for to me. Alexus was who I wanted. Just thinking about her made me want to talk to her. I grabbed my phone and dialed her number.

"Hey," she answered on the third ring.

"Where are you? I'm trying to see you today." I knew that I was supposed to be going somewhere with Cherika and the kids, but I would cancel if I had to.

"I don't think I'll be able to. I have my nieces and nephew," she replied. I automatically assumed she was lying, so I went off.

"You gon' stop trying to put me on the back burner for that nigga! You're starting to piss me off with that shit!"

"I'm not even with him right now. I'm babysitting my nieces and nephew. You always think somebody is lying to you!"

"That's because you're always lying."

"I'm not lying. Me and Jada are about to bring them somewhere," she replied. I should have known that her sidekick was back in the picture. She couldn't stay away too long.

"Well, what time are y'all coming back? I'm not waiting until tomorrow; I want to see you today."

"I'm not making any promises, but I'll see if I can get away later. You're getting on my damn nerves," she said, sounding aggravated.

I was about to say something else, but I didn't hear her background anymore. I looked at the phone and noticed that she'd hung up on me. I swear, I couldn't wait until I was home for good. I planned on giving her and her new man a run for their money.

Two hours later, we were pulling into a parking spot at the zoo. I was already kicking myself for letting Cherika spend the day with us. She was on some family day bullshit and I was not trying to hear it. Since I talked to Alexus earlier, I was in a foul mood. I tried to call her back, but she was sending me straight to voicemail with her childish ass.

"Let's take a picture," Cherika said, pulling out her cellphone. She was out of her damn mind if she thought that she was posting a picture of me on Facebook or Instagram.

"Man, I'm not taking no pictures. Let's go."

I grabbed Drew and Lil Dre's hand and started walking towards the entrance. The sooner I got this over with, the sooner I could get rid of her aggravating ass. Besides, I wanted to catch up with Alexus before it got too late.

"Maybe we can go get some pizza when we leave here." Cherika looked at me and I wanted to slap that stupid ass smirk off of her face.

My kids were getting happy about the idea, but I shot it down before it went too far.

"No, I'll order y'all some pizza when I drop y'all off at home."

Her ass was always trying to be slick. I felt sorry for her earlier, but I wasn't falling for it this time. I paid the fee for us to get into the zoo and we all made our way through the gate. I rented a wagon for Drew and Lil Dre just in case they got tired of walking. We let the kids decide where they wanted to go first and we were on our way. Even though Cherika and I were separated, it felt good doing something as a family. She was alright as long as she wasn't being loud and common.

Just as I expected, a little over an hour into our walk, Drew and Lil Dre were in the wagon knocked out. Cherika wanted to sit down, but Denim and Dream were still amped. Sitting down was out of the question for them. They were pulling me by both hands, trying to get me to accompany them to see the snakes.

"I'm about to take them to see the snakes. You want to sit here until I come back?" I asked Cherika, pointing to a sitting area to our left.

"Yeah, I'll meet y'all in there once I rest up for a minute," she replied.

I grabbed both of my daughters' hands and led them to the enclosed area that housed about one hundred snakes. I hated snakes, so I started frowning as soon as we walked into the dark exhibit room. My daughters were the exact opposite. They appeared to be mesmerized as they made their way around the spacious room. I followed them every step of the way, making sure to keep an eye on them both.

"Daddy, I know her," Denim said, pointing across the room. I looked in the direction that she was pointing in, but I couldn't make out who she was pointing at.

"Who?" I asked, still looking in that direction. It was kind of dark, so it was hard for me to see.

"That lady right there, I know her," Denim said, running away from me.

"Girl, come back here!" I yelled as I ran behind her, holding onto Dream's hand.

She ran around to the other side of the room and started yelling in excitement. "Alexus!" I heard the name that she called and I got just as excited as she was.

When I finally caught up with her, I saw Alexus kneeling to give her a hug. Dream let go of my hand and ran over to greet her as well.

"See daddy, I told you that I know that lady," Denim said, pointing to Jada.

I guess Alexus wasn't lying about babysitting. She had her nieces and nephew standing right next to her. I was just as happy to see her as my girls were. I walked up to her and kissed her on the lips, despite the look of hate that was coming from Jada. I grabbed Lex by the hand and pulled her into a dark corner. I wanted a real kiss and I didn't need her hating ass friend in my business.

"Jada, keep an eye on them for me," she said, walking away with me.

I picked her small frame up and pinned her against the wall. She wrapped her arms around my neck right before I shoved my tongue down her throat. We kissed for what felt like forever. I really wished I didn't have to let her go but, eventually, I did.

"I told you that I wasn't lying about babysitting," she said, looking at me.

"I see that. I'm sorry baby," I replied softly.

Damn, I was in love with this girl. It was killing me to know that she was probably in love with somebody else.

"So, am I going to see you later?" I asked her. She looked away and I just knew that I wasn't going to like her reply.

"I don't know if I can. I already promised Tyree that I would go to the movies with him tonight."

"Man, fuck Tyree!" I shouted in anger. *What kind of fucking name is that anyway?* I said to myself.

"Shhh. That's Jada's cousin, so stop talking so loud," she whispered.

"Man, fuck her too!"

"Let me go Dre," she said, breaking our embrace. "I knew that hooking up with you again was a bad idea."

196

"No, it ain't a bad idea. You're just worried about ole boy finding out. Stop acting like that nigga is God or something."

She was really starting to piss me off with this boyfriend of hers. I almost forgot all about being here with Cherika and my kids until I heard her voice.

"Where's your daddy?" I heard her ask my girls. Alexus looked over at me with fire in her eyes and my heart dropped. I was barely in good with her and things weren't getting any better.

"You're here with your wife?" she asked through clenched teeth.

"It's not even like that."

"You're in here going off on me about spending time with my man, but you're in here with your wife. Nigga, fuck you; lose my number." She turned around and walked off with me hot on her heels.

Cherika looked like she saw a ghost when she saw us both come from the corner that we were ducked off in. She dropped her purse and charged at Lex, full speed.

"Bitch, I wish you would," Lex said, while looking Cherika up and down. I jumped in front of her to prevent any licks from being thrown.

"Don't try to protect that slut!" Cherika yelled. People were starting to look at us as if we were the ones on display. Lex grabbed her nieces and nephew and walked off with Jada in tow.

"I see you must really want me to kill you and that bitch," Cherika said angrily.

I looked in her eyes and knew that she was dead ass serious.

"I'm coming right back," I said, quickly walking away.

197

"You better not be going run behind that hoe. Are you really that stupid?"

I ignored her and kept going. I spotted Lex and her crew walking towards the exit. I did a slow jog until I caught up with them.

"Lex, wait." I grabbed her arm to stop her.

"Don't touch me, Dre. You are never going to change. I really feel sorry for your wife because she married a straight up dog."

"It's not even like that. You act like I knew that you were going to be here."

"That's not the point!".

"Well, then, what is the point?" I yelled in frustration.

"That's the point," she said, pointing behind me.

I turned around and saw Cherika and my kids walking towards me. Lex grabbed her nieces' hands and continued walking away. I expected Cherika to say something, but she surprised me when she didn't. She walked right pass me, going towards the same exit as Alexus. I immediately started following her to make sure she wasn't on no bullshit.

"Cherika, don't come out here acting a fool," I said, walking close behind her.

"Don't worry; I'm not trying to do nothing to your bitch. I'm just ready to go home," she replied calmly.

She was a little too calm for me and that was kind of scary. We continued to walk in silence until we made it to the car. I looked around, but I didn't see Alexus nowhere in sight.

I opened the doors and started helping the kids get into the car. Cherika was just standing there with a far-off look on her face.

"What are you just standing there for?" I asked as I walked up to her.

"I can't take this anymore Dre. I feel like I'm losing my mind over this foolishness. Why would you tell her to come here when we're supposed to be spending time with our kids?"

"I didn't tell her to come here. I didn't even know that she was going to be here."

"I don't believe you. I just can't see both of y'all showing up to the same place at the same time."

"You can believe what you want, but I'm telling you I didn't know that she was going to be here. Let's go. It's too hot to be standing out here." I walked around to the driver's side of the car, but she didn't move.

"Cherika, let's go. I'm not for your bullshit today!" She was just standing there, looking off into space.

"She really is losing her mind," I mumbled to myself. "Cherika!" I yelled her name again, but she still didn't move. I walked back over to her and tapped her on the shoulder.

"This is never going to end, is it?"

"What are you talking about? What's never going to end?" She was talking crazy and I didn't have time for that shit.

"You and her, it's never going to end," she said, looking at me with tears rolling down her cheeks. I was getting sick and tired of all this damn crying. If it wasn't her crying, it was Alexus.

"Cherika, let's go. It's hot, my kids are ready to go, and so am I."

She hesitated for a minute, but she finally started walking to the car. She came to her senses at just the right time because her ass was about to get left. I drove off, silently thanking God that nothing popped off between her and Alexus.

I looked over at Cherika as she stared out the window, looking at nothing in particular. Keeping her around was proving to be more work than it was worth. Maybe I needed to rethink this divorce thing and let her go her way.

Chapter 24

It'd been about two weeks since I got fired from one job and started working at another. She She's was a popular strip club located in New Orleans East. My ex co-worker, Lisa, got me on over there, but I wasn't making any real money yet. I was the new girl, so I had to go in on the early shift. The crowd didn't really get there until midnight and I was always gone by then. Lisa promised me that she would get me on the later shift but, so far, nothing had happened. She said that it would be any day now, so all I had to do was wait.

I'd finally found the courage to tell Troy about my new occupation. I thought that he was going to flip, but he was surprisingly calm about it. He even said that he wanted to come see me dance when he got out, which would be any day now.

Malik was another story. According to him, only whores took their clothes off for money. I wondered what it was called when it was done for free because that's exactly what I was doing with his broke ass. I really didn't care about what anybody had to say. My bills were being paid and I wasn't starving.

Grabbing my purse and cellphone, I headed out the door to run a few errands before it was time for me to be at the club. My cousin, Eric, worked at Firestone, so I was going there to get the oil changed on my car. I hated going there, but I couldn't pass up anything that was free. I pulled up to the entrance and sent Eric a text, letting him know that my car was up front with the keys still inside. I always sat in the cool waiting room until he finished doing what he had to do. As soon as I stepped inside the room, I was met with a glorious sight.

"Hey, you," I said, speaking to Tyree. He had his head down, looking through a car magazine. I hadn't been seeing him too much since I lost my job.

"What's up?" he spoke back with a nod of his head.

He was too damn cute. That hoe Alexus did not deserve him. She had her pick of two fine men, but her selfish ass wanted them both. I thought back to how she played me in the store the last time I saw her and my blood started to boil. The wheels in my head started turning and that was never good for the other person when that happened. Being the vindictive person that I was, there was no way in hell I was letting Alexus get away with talking to me like I was beneath her. I was sitting there thinking of how I wanted to tell Tyree what was going on without actually looking like the bad girl. I didn't know how long he was going to be in here, so I had to act fast.

"Sorry to hear about you and Alexus breaking up. Y'all made such a cute couple," I said in my most sincere voice.

He looked up from the magazine, and I knew right then and there that I had his full attention.

"Who told you that we broke up?" he asked, tossing the magazine aside.

"Nobody, I just assumed y'all did when I saw her with..." I stopped talking mid-sentence. "Never mind, I'm talking too much."

Judging from the look on his face, I had him right where I wanted him.

"No, you're not talking too much. Who did you see her with?" he asked, sounding upset. I hesitated like I didn't want tell him. He was looking at me like he was ready for me to answer his question, so I did just that.

"Well, I was in the mall the other day and I saw her in there with my cousin, Dre. I just figured y'all broke up and they were back together."

Maybe it was my imagination, but I could have sworn that I saw the veins in his neck jumping. He was heated. The sparks were about to fly. I just wished I was around when it did. He nodded his head and picked up his magazine. He tried to play it off, but he was deep in thought about the news he'd just received.

"Taylor," the clerk said from behind the desk. I made it just under the buzzer. Tyree stood up and walked over to the counter. I watched him the entire time, thinking of how we would look together. Despite what Alexus thought, we would make a beautiful couple and I was not giving up on it.

Once he paid his bill and got his keys, Tyree headed for the exit but stopped before he left. He turned around and walked back to where I was sitting.

"I thought you said that your cousin was in jail," he said while looking down at me.

"He was. I didn't even know that he was home until I saw them in the mall."

Actually, I'd found out from Eric that Dre was released from the program that he was in a few days ago. He was out on a weekend pass when I saw him parked outside the mall.

"What day was that you saw them together?"

"Let's step outside and talk."

I got up from my seat and walked away. Tyree followed me out of the building and into the parking lot. If he was willing to hear it, I was willing to tell it all.

Later on that night, I was getting prepared to go to the club. I was in a great mood. Not only did Tyree and I talk for over an hour earlier, but I finally got the call that I'd been waiting for. Lisa was able to get me on the late shift at the club. I was a little nervous, even though she assured me that everything would be fine. I was used to the small crowd that came in early, but the late shift always danced to a full house. From what I heard from Lisa; the money was triple what I made on the early shift. With the tip money I made, I was able to get a few new outfits to dance in and they were all on point.

After locking my apartment door, I hopped in my car and made my way over to the club. My nerves were shot because I didn't know what to expect. I didn't have the best body in the world, but it wasn't the worst either. If I decided to make a career out of this stripping thing, I would definitely take the steps to enhance some things that I didn't like about myself. For one, I would make my ass bigger than the small handful that it was now. Troy always made me feel bad because of that.

After my twenty-minute drive, I pulled up to the club and parked my car around back. I grabbed my duffel bag and made my way through the dancer's entrance. Looking around the small, cluttered room, I didn't recognize any of the faces that stood before me. Some of the girls looked me up and down and turned their heads, not bothering to speak. I tried looking for Lisa, but I didn't see her anywhere in the room.

"You must be the new girl that Lisa was telling me about?" a tall, slender woman asked me.

"Yeah, I'm Keanna," I replied.

"I'm Ayanna, but just call me Yonnie. Let me show you me and Lisa's spot," she said, leading me further into the room.

I'd been here plenty of times before tonight, but everything looked so different now. I followed Yonnie to a small corner in the room that I'd never noticed before. They had two long mirrors on the wall and a small vanity against the wall.

"First thing you need to know is you don't have any friends around here. These hoes are out for themselves. If you need anything, just come to me or Lisa. Here, you're going to need this." Yonnie handed me a small bottle of liquor.

"Ok, thanks. Is Lisa here yet?"

"Yeah, she's here. Some of her regulars wanted to see her, but she'll be back. Until another one becomes available, you can put your things in my locker."

I'd just met Ayanna, but I liked her already. She was going out of her way to make sure that I was straight.

"You can start changing into your dance clothes. We'll be going out in a little while," Ayanna said.

She pulled her shirt over her head and began to undress. I was still nervous, so I just sat there and watched.

"I know you're not scared. It's not like this is your first time doing this." She laughed but she was right. I was terrified.

"No, but I'm not used to working a full house. There was hardly anyone in here when I worked the early shift."

"Yeah but you don't make any money either. I have three kids, so I need all the tips I can get."

I really took a good look at Ayanna. She was a very pretty girl. Her stomach was flat, so I wouldn't have thought that she had three kids. I also noticed that, just like me, she wasn't working with much from behind. I guess if she could do it, then so could I.

"Girl, it's on and popping out there," Lisa said, walking over to us. "I see you made it girl. Hurry up and change, so you can get some of that money they throwing around."

Yonnie stripped down out of everything that she had on and started putting on her dance clothes. I didn't mean to be so obvious, but I couldn't help but stare at her slender frame.

"Like what you see?" she asked, smiling at me.

I lowered my head in embarrassment.

"Don't be scared to look; I'm not." She winked at me and I smiled. If I didn't know any better, I would think that she was flirting with me. If she only knew that I was definitely up for the challenge.

Lisa left us alone to get dressed while she went back out on the floor.

"I'm going to peep out front, but I won't go out until you're done," Yonnie announced.

"Good, I don't want to go out there by myself."

206

Once Yonnie walked away, I got undressed and began to put on my dance clothes. I lightly applied some make-up to my face and slipped into my stilettos. Looking myself over in the mirror, I smiled at my reflection. My royal blue boy shorts and midriff halter looked great on me. The royal and silver shoes I wore made the outfit pop even more. I opened the small bottle of liquor that Yonnie gave me and downed the entire bottle. The liquor burned like hell going down, but I needed it to calm my nerves.

"Fuck!" Yonnie screamed when she walked back into the dressing room. She yanked her locker open and pulled out her duffel bag.

"Are you alright?" I asked, walking up to her.

"Hell no, I'm not alright. I'm getting my shit and going back home," she said angrily. I got nervous when she said that. I was depending on her to show me the ropes of the night shift.

"Why, what happened?"

"My sister's ex-boyfriend is out there. There's no way in hell I'm going out there and dance in front of that nigga!"

"Damn, that's messed up." I didn't know what else to say to her.

"I hate Dre's punk ass. The only thing he's going to do is call that uppity bitch and tell her my business."

Did she just say Dre? I thought to myself. "What Dre?" I asked, walking over to her.

"You don't know him, trust me. You're not his type."

"Don't be too sure. What's your sister's name?"

"You don't know who I'm talking about so stop asking me all these damn questions!"

Just that fast, I'd put the puzzle together. Ayanna was Alexus' sister. I'd never met her before today, but that name did ring a bell. I remembered Alexus always being at her house.

"Is your sister named Alexus?"

"Yeah, how did you know?"

"Dre is my first cousin. I'm friends with Jada and Lex. Well, I use to be anyway."

"Fuck both of them hoes!"

"It looks like you and I have a lot in common. I can't stand them bitches either. They did me so wrong, it's ridiculous," I lied.

I proceeded to tell Yonnie all about the failed friendship between the three of us while she shared her story with me in return. It appeared that Alexus wasn't the only thing that we had in common. Jada appeared to be getting around a lot lately. My heart wasn't the only one that she'd broken.

"Well, Dre is not her ex. I know for a fact that she's still dealing with him. I saw it with my own eyes," I informed Ayanna.

"Well, I know for a fact that she's still dealing with Tyree too. I hope her ass gets busted."

"That's not hard to make happen. Let me put my clothes back on. If my cousin is out there then I'm not dancing either," I said, standing to my feet. I had a plan, but I needed some help to pull it off.

Once I was dressed, I told Ayanna what was on my mind. She assured me that she was definitely on board with whatever I did, so that was good to hear. Getting Dre on board was going to be a hard task. I had to pitch my idea in a way that was beneficial to him.

"I guess we need to go out there and talk to Dre. If he's on board, it'll be all good from there," I said to Yonnie.

"Dre and I don't have the best relationship. You might want to do all the talking."

"It won't be any better if I do it. Thanks to your sister, we don't really get along like we use to."

She didn't need to know the real reason that Dre and I fell out.

"Well, let's get this over with."

She led the way out of the dressing room with me following right behind her. We bobbed and weaved around a crowd of men until we came to the table where Dre, Eric, and a few of their friends were seated. Eric was the first to notice us and he made our presence known.

"Keanna, what the hell are you doing in the strip club?" he asked, while looking Ayanna up and down lustfully. When Dre heard my name, he almost choked on the beer that he was drinking.

"What the fuck are you doing here? And what the fuck is she doing here with you?" Dre looked from me to Ayanna.

"We wanted to holler at you about something," I replied nervously.

"Girl, if you don't get your ass away from this table. Y'all must be crazy," he said, waving us off.

"Wait, y'all don't have to rush off. Pull up a chair and talk to me for a minute sweetheart." Eric was flirting with Ayanna.

"Bruh, don't even waste your time with that one; she's cheering for the other team now." Dre laughed at his own joke.

"Fuck you, Dre," Ayanna spat angrily.

"Fuck you too. Hating ass bitch."

209

"Forget it Keanna. I can't deal with his arrogant ass. Don't even worry about it." She walked away but I grabbed her arm to stop her from leaving.

"Wait, don't leave. Just don't say anything, let me do all the talking." I was desperately trying to regain control of the situation. I grabbed a chair and motioned for her to take a seat. After she sat down, I pulled out another chair and moved it closer to Dre.

"What part of get the fuck away from me didn't you understand?" Dre asked, looking me dead in my eyes.

"Just give me five minutes of your time. If you still want me to leave once I'm done talking, I'll respect your wishes."

"I don't understand what we could possibly have to talk about. I really don't want to hear nothing that you have to say." He turned his head and took a sip of his beer.

"Even if it's about Alexus?" I asked. I knew that curiosity would get the best of him and I was right.

"Start talking. You got five minutes," he said, giving me his undivided attention.

Ayanna and I spent over twenty minutes running everything down to him. He was in, and all we had to do was get the ball rolling. I was about to make Alexus regret the day that she ever decided to cross me, and Ayanna felt the same way.

Chapter 25

I hadn't been in the best mood lately. My work load was crazy, so I barely had any free time to spend with Alexus. Lately, all we'd been doing was arguing because I was never really home. That and the fact that my trust in her was almost non-existent.

Since running into Keanna a few weeks ago, I'd been questioning everything that Alexus told me. I was never the insecure type, but I felt like she was hiding something from me. It didn't help that she was always so defensive whenever I asked her about it. I didn't want to believe that she was doing something wrong, but all the signs were pointing right to it.

In all the years that I'd been dating, I could only recall my heart being broken once by someone who I didn't love half as much as I loved Alexus. I didn't like the place that we were in and I was ready to do something about it.

I decided to schedule all of my appointments for the next two mornings so I would be free to spend all my nights at home with her. It was going to be hard on me, but my girl was definitely worth it. I was excited to be pulling up to my last appointment of the day. It was a small medical supply company that we leased a building to in Laplace, Louisiana. They were unsure about renewing their lease, so it was my job to make sure they did. Dressed casually in some slacks and a button down, I entered the building, ready to get down to business. I ignored the lustful stares from the female employees and made my way to the second-floor board room.

An hour later, I was leaving my meeting with another signed five-year lease. My pops was going to be happy to hear that. I pulled my phone out of my pocket as I headed back to my car. I wanted to call Alexus to confirm our plans for the night. Before I got a chance to do so, I spotted someone walking across the parking lot.

"What's up Alex?" I spoke to Alexus' brother. He walked towards me with his hand extended for me to shake it.

"Hey, what are you doing all the way out here in the country?" he asked.

"I had to attend a meeting in the building," I said, pointing to the structure behind me.

"Ok, that's where I work."

"Oh, I didn't know that."

"You and Lex are still together, huh?"

"Yeah, we're still hanging in there," I replied with a smile.

"That's what's up. I'm happy to hear that. She needs a good man in her life." He nodded his head in approval.

"Well, I got to get to work, so I won't hold you up. Tell my sister that I'll probably come see them this weekend; it's been a minute since we saw each other."

That was strange because according to Alexus, she'd been by her brother's house quite often during the past couple of weeks.

"When's the last time you saw her?" I was curious to know.

"It's been a minute, probably over two months now. I know my mama is going to curse me out for staying away so long. They refuse to come out here, so I always have to go to them."

My heart dropped when he was done talking. Alexus had straight up lied to me and her brother had just confirmed it. I tried to do the right thing and trust Alexus, but that was a done deal.

"Alright then, it was nice seeing you again. Maybe I'll see you when you come over," I said, giving him dap.

Alex and I said our goodbyes and I was on my way soon after. I hated to admit that Keanna could possibly be right about Alexus being unfaithful, but it was staring me right in my face. If she wasn't staying at her brother's house when we broke up, then where was she? I knew for a fact that she wasn't at Jada's or her mother's houses because I checked several times. Getting the truth from Alexus was never going to happen and I knew that for sure. Looking down at my phone, I did something that I promised myself I wouldn't do, no matter what happened; I called Keanna.

Chapter 26

Dre had been blowing my phone up for the past few days. I'd been trying to do right by Tyree and leave him alone, but he was making things too hard. After I ran into him and his family at the zoo, I decided that I was done with him for good. But, just like every other time, Dre had ways of making me change my mind. Four days after that incident, we ended up picking up right where we left off. He was happy about us reconnecting, but I was having second thoughts the moment it started again. I still had feelings for Dre, but they were lust and not love. I was really in love with Tyree. If I had to choose between the two, Dre wouldn't stand a chance.

Lately, Tyree and I hadn't been in the best place with our relationship, but we were working hard to get it back on track. He'd been questioning me a lot lately and I really think he was becoming suspicious. That was the reason why I'd been putting Dre on the back burner lately. I wasn't trying to make matters worse with me and my man, so Dre had to wait until I was able to make time for him. He was having a fit, but I didn't give a damn.

Tyree was working hard to make earlier appointments so that we could spend some much-needed time together. Things we're going good for the first few days, but he was back to becoming suspicious again. He never came right out and asked, but I could tell that he had doubts, just by some of the things he said. Then, to make matters worse, Tyree and his dad had to attend a two-day seminar in Houston, Texas. I waited for him to ask me to join them, but the invite never came.

"Girl, I really needed this," Jada said as she placed her feet in the warm water.

We were both at a local nail salon getting pedicures.

"I did too," I replied, agreeing with her. "I'm so aggravated with Tyree right now."

"I don't know why you're so mad about him not inviting you out of town. You have class, so you probably couldn't go anyway."

"That's not the point. He didn't even ask. I could have made arrangements for school."

"Y'all need a vacation. Just get away and have some alone time," Jada suggested.

"I don't know; I'm stressed the hell out."

"We did say no more secrets, right?" Jada looked at me suspiciously.

"Why, are you hiding something else from me?"

"No, but I have to be honest with you."

"Ok, I'm listening."

"You're stressed out because you're trying to please two men at the same time. You need to let Dre go for good and be with Tyree if that's who you really want to be with. I don't see this turning out good at all."

"I do want to be with Tyree, but you know that Dre is not just going to just go away that easily."

"No, he's not, because you're entertaining him. You're doing my cousin the same thing that he's doing to his wife and it's not going to turn out good."

I was listening because Jada had some very good points, but the situations were different.

"No, I'm not. Unlike Dre, I want to be with Tyree. Dre just doesn't want to be married anymore."

"Ok, so why isn't he divorced? That's bullshit. He's keeping her around for a reason, but she's going to really get tired one day. A person can only take so much. I'm scared for you more than anything," Jada said seriously.

"I'm not worrying about Cherika's crazy ass. If anything, she'll do him something before me. He's the one that married her dumb ass."

"That girl is crazy. She faults you for everything that happened with her husband, so don't think she wouldn't come after you before she goes after Dre."

"I know. I really do have to end this with him. I feel like I have much more to lose than Dre. It's not even worth it."

That was so true. I would die if Tyree found out that I was still messing with Dre, especially since I swore that it was over between us.

"Well, I've said what was on my mind. I just don't trust Dre at all. He'll do anything for you to be with him. Just be careful is all I'm saying."

"I will." I heard her loud and clear. Hearing was never my issue; it was listening that gave me the most problems.

After our trip to the nail salon, I headed straight to Tyree's house. He would be leaving tomorrow and I wasn't going to see him for the entire weekend. I wanted to spend some time with him before he left. Not wanting to be alone, I made plans to spend the weekend with Jada at her house.

"Hey boo," I said when I walked into Tyree's house. He was stretched out on the sofa watching tv. I walked over to him, giving him a peck on his lips.

"What you been up to today?" he asked, while pulling me down on top of him.

"Nothing, I just came from the nail salon with Jada."

We laid on the sofa in silence for over an hour watching reruns of Martin, until Tyree initiated a conversation.

"Are you happy?" he asked out of the blue.

The question caught me of guard, but I answered truthfully.

"I'm very happy, are you?"

"Yeah, I'm happy." He was quiet for a while, but more questions came soon after his brief silence.

"If you weren't happy, would you tell me?"

"Yes, I would tell you, Tyree. Where is all of this coming from?"

"I'm just asking. I just want to make sure that I'm doing what I'm supposed to do to make you happy. If you're not happy with me, then you'll start to look elsewhere and I don't want that to happen."

"That's not going to happen." I felt like shit and for good reason. Tyree was a good man and I didn't have a valid reason to cheat on him. It really was only about the sex with Dre, but it wasn't like Tyree wasn't putting it down just as good, maybe even better. Our sex life was damn good and I didn't have any complaints. Since he'd been coming in early for the past few nights, we'd been making up for lost times.

"If this is not what you want, just let me know. I don't want to keep you if you don't want to be kept," he said, surprising me.

"I don't understand where all of this is coming from. You're not forcing me to be here. I'm here because I love you and this is where I want to be," I replied, looking him in his eyes.

"I love you too. Please don't make me regret it."

That last comment sealed the deal. This weekend, while Tyree was out of town working, I would be working on ending whatever it was that I had with Dre. The risk was just too great. Tyree and I shared a long kiss right before he picked me up and carried me up the stairs. Starting tonight, he was the only man that I would be sharing my body with.

The next morning, I got up extra early to make sure that Tyree had packed everything he needed. I was still tired since we stayed up until after two. Tyree's sex drive was most definitely out of control. It was Friday, so I only had one class at eleven. I also had a three-hour class on Saturday, which was probably the reason he didn't ask me to join him on the trip in the first place. Tyree was very serious about school, so skipping class was not happening.

Once I made sure that he had everything he needed, I got dressed and prepared to leave out the door at the same time he was leaving. Jada and I were going to have breakfast with the twins before it was time for me to go to school.

"You sure you don't want to stay here until I get back?" he asked for the hundredth time.

"No, I told you that I was staying with Jada. I don't want to be in here bored for the whole weekend," I answered.

We walked out the door together and prepared to go our separate ways. After putting his bags in the car, Tyree lifted me off my feet in a tight embrace. After sharing a long kiss, he pulled himself away and got in his car. I hopped in mine as well and headed to breakfast with my girls.

Later on Friday night, Jada and I sat around in her living room and pigged out on junk food all night while watching movies. Tyree called to let me know that he and his dad had made it to Texas safely, and I was happy to hear that. He was tired from driving all day, so he promised to call me on Saturday evening once they were done with all their meetings.

"Is that your stalker calling you again?" Jada asked laughing.

Dre had been calling me nonstop since earlier today. I talked to him briefly, just to let him know that I didn't want to continue what we had. He wasn't trying to hear it, so he'd been trying to get in touch with me all day.

"Yeah, that's his disgusting ass," I replied, silencing my phone once again.

"You need to just answer for him. You already said what you had to say. He just needs to accept it and move on."

"Girl, forget Dre; let's find something else for us to watch," I said while flipping through some channels.

We settled on a Lifetime movie and continued to enjoy our night. About ten minutes into the movie, my phone started going off again. Instead of ignoring it, I decided to pick up this time.

"What Dre?" I asked in an annoyed tone. He was getting on my nerves and I was ready for him to stop calling. The only reason I didn't turn the phone off was because I didn't want to miss a call from Tyree.

"Open the door," he said right before he disconnected the call.

"What did he say?" Jada asked.

"He said to open the door," I replied.

"How the hell did he even know that you were here? This nigga is a stalker for real," Jada said while walking to the door.

"He must have seen my car outside," I replied while walking to the door with her.

Being his usual arrogant self, Dre walked right past Jada as soon as the door was opened.

"Excuse you. You need to speak when you walk into my house," Jada said with her hand on her hip.

"Hey Jada," he replied, sounding irritated. He looked over at me and walked further into the living room.

"Let me talk to you for a minute," he said while looking down at me.

"Y'all can go upstairs in the other bedroom if you want to," Jada said to me.

Without waiting for me, Dre walked off and headed upstairs to the room. He knew this house inside and out since he'd been here so many times before. I started walking behind him, but Jada pulled me back before I got too far.

221

"Hurry up and get rid of his ass. I don't want to be put in the middle of this mess. Tyree is going to kill me if he finds out that I let him in my house."

"I know. I'm sorry, but I didn't know that he was going to show up here."

I took the steps two at a time, trying to get to Dre. I wanted him to say what he had to say and leave just as quickly as he came. He was sitting on the bed playing with his phone when I entered the room.

"Why are you here Dre? I told you that I was done with this and I meant it," I said, standing near the door.

"So, just like that, you don't want to have nothing to do with me anymore? What did I do this time?"

"You didn't do anything Dre. I told you that I'm just trying to make things right with Tyree." I wasn't trying to hurt his feelings, but I had to be honest. I couldn't do this anymore.

"Why is everything always about him now? I hope he's as loyal to you as you are to him."

"He's my boyfriend; that's why everything is always about him. And don't even try to use that reverse psychology on me."

"So, you expect me to walk away just like that?" he asked, walking towards me.

I thought he was leaving, so I moved to the side, allowing him to pass. Instead of walking out of the room, he closed the door and stood in front of it. I thought back to what Jada said about Dre doing anything for me, and I got scared. I didn't think that Dre would ever hurt me, but I couldn't be too sure. When a person's back was against the wall, anything was possible.

"Dre, please don't do this. You need to just leave." I was nervous and I didn't try to hide it.

222

He ignored me and pushed me down on the bed, laying his tall muscular frame on top of me. I tried hard not to, but I couldn't resist the scent of his Ralph Lauren cologne. When he pinned my arms up above my head, I tried to protest, but it was too late. He covered my lips with his and all my words were silenced. This was not supposed to be happening. Not only was I about to have sex with my married ex-boyfriend, but I was doing it in the home of my current boyfriend's cousin. Jada would kill me if she knew what was going on.

After a long passionate kiss, Dre stood up and started to remove his clothes. If I wanted to stop him, now was the time. Instead, I looked on as he took off every piece of clothing that he had on. When he was done, he walked over to the bed and proceeded to do the same thing with me. Still, I never attempted to stop him. Once we were both undressed, he got up to turn off the light before rejoining me in the bed. As soon as he got back in the bed, he did what he usually did to make me forget why I wanted to break up with him in the first place. He pushed my legs back as far as they could go before burying his entire face in between my legs.

A few hours later, I woke up feeling slightly overheated. It took a few minutes for me to get my bearings and realize where I was. I tried to sit up, but a pair of strong arms prevented me from doing so. I looked at the clock and almost died when I saw that it was after two in the morning. Dre was knocked out, still just as naked as the day he was born. I tried to pry his arms from around my naked body, but that only made him hold me tighter. I really needed him to wake up and make his exit before Jada noticed that he was still here. Just as I was about nudge him, I heard Jada's voice coming from downstairs.

"How the hell did y'all get in here? Get out before I call the police!" she yelled.

"Dre, get up" I said, while shaking him at the same time.

I didn't know who Jada was talking to and I was scared. I thought someone had broken into the house and I wanted to

223

make sure that my friend was alright. I heard some more voices, but I couldn't make out who they belonged to.

"Dre, get up! Something is going on downstairs," I said in a panic.

"Girl, go back to sleep. You must be having a bad dream," he said, sounding groggy.

"No, I'm not, just listen."

The voices were getting louder and it sounded like they were coming up the stairs.

"Please don't do this. Just listen for a minute," Jada was pleading.

"I know you heard that," I said, looking at Dre.

Both of us sat straight up in the bed just as the bedroom door flew open. I grabbed the cover and pulled it over me and Dre's naked bodies. I was in panic mode until the lights came on and I saw who it was standing in the doorway.

"I knew that you were a hoe," Keanna said, standing there smiling.

Ayanna was standing right next to her, shaking her head with that stupid ass smirk on her face. Jada pushed past both of them and stood at the foot of the bed crying.

"Lex, I'm so sorry. I don't know how they got in here," she said crying from the pit of her stomach.

I didn't know what the hell Jada was crying for. It didn't matter to me if they knew about me and Dre. It was my word against theirs and I was taking this to my grave. She had nothing to be sorry about.

I was just about to go off when another shadow appeared from the darkened hallway. I knew the expression on my face had to be the same as a deer caught in the headlights. My heart dropped at a quickened pace and my words were caught in my throat when I looked up and locked eyes with Tyree...